KILLING CONGRESS

GEOFF CRATCH

Also by Geoff Cratch

Beneath the Shadow of

the Cross

DEDICATION

Betsy and I dedicate this story to our children, their spouses, our grandchildren and great grandchildren:

Stephanie Cratch Hall
    John Gabriel Hall, EmmaLee West Hall.
        Kylie Rose Hall, Emery Asher Hall.
    Devynn Brooke Hall, Georgia Grace Hall, Josiah Jordan Hall.
Courtney Cratch Foster, Larry Ray Foster
    Geoffrey Ray Foster
    Bradley Michael Foster, Holly Matzker Foster.
        Bailey Rae Foster, Hadley Elizabeth Foster, Brody Daniel Foster, Hayden Joy Foster
    Malaney Courtlyn Foster, Ruby Elise Foster, Timothy Arion Foster, Nathan Isaiah Foster, Lily Nicole Foster.
Julie Cratch Mihill, Timothy Mark Mihill.
    Sara Jewel Mihill Santmier, Nicholas Eli Santmier
        Nicholas Eli Santmier, II
    Jake Dakota Mihill, Jared Burke Mihill, Joshua Mark Mihill, Jonah Luke Mihill, James Alexander Mihill and Jadon Timothy Mihill.

You are all loved, prayed for and considered a real blessing to Gramma and me.

PROLOGUE

THE DEATH OF the first United States Congressman occurred on February 7, 2018, and unfortunately, over the next four weeks, several more Congressmen would also be murdered. The bizarre nature of the ensuing events had us chasing terrorists, political zealots, religious fanatics and kept us wondering if the murders were connected or not.

When it was over, I realized that this story needs telling so that people will see the perils our nation faces if we continue down the path we are on. Politically, we are so divided that our enemies are laughing at us as we commit national suicide. We must begin to see our two-party system as being on the same team, like the offense and the defense, rather than two separate teams. If we do not start working together to create a better government and stop hating each other for our differing views, this democracy will come tumbling down around our necks.

There is an evil force amongst us that is deliberately trying to bring America to its knees. Stay tuned for you may find that you have been unwittingly drawn into its' evil clutches.

I chose to take a leave of absence from the FBI and to use my daily journals to bring you this story, as quickly as possible. The most fitting title of my story must be, Killing Congress. If we do not reverse the course we are on, someone will write the next book and call it Killing America."

CHAPTER 1

LET ME INTRODUCE myself: I am Colton, shortened to Colt so long ago I don't remember to whom blame is due, McLean. Born November 23, 1978, do the math, just turned 40 years of age. Single, not by choice but by accident, white male. My wife was killed by a reckless driver on the D.C. beltway five years ago. Since then I have become a workaholic, devoting all my time and attention to my duties as a Special Agent for the Federal Bureau of Investigation. Now assigned to the Counter Intelligence Division and working out of an office in Crystal City, Virginia.

For the benefit of those of you who have not watched the national news of late, where you would most definitely have seen me. Others most often describe me as six feet two inches tall, two hundred and forty pounds, black hair, with a touch of gray at the temples, blue eyes and I usually have a 5 o'clock shadow due to my heavy beard.

Things that you cannot see by looking at me include a tender heart that will betray me to the point of tears when I see or hear tender, loving or even tragic things. The scar of losing my wife after our short marriage and not having the opportunity to be a father has left its mark. And I am just now beginning to realize that my obsession with work has robbed me of all social life. I have hardly looked at another woman since Grace died nor have I had a night out with the boys. Only in the last two years have I

gradually returned to my religious roots, going to church maybe once a month. I now am being pulled back to God by His great love and have just committed to becoming more focused on those around me who need to know Him.

So, the story that I feel led to bring to you begins on February 6, 2018, as I sit in my cubicle going over my extensive notes from several still pending cases, desperately looking for something that would help move us closer to solving situations with serious national security implications. I was thinking how grateful I am that my friend and mentor, Dave Rowlands, had instilled in me on my first job after graduating from the FBI Academy at Quantico, the necessity of keeping copious notes on my daily activities. Taking extensive notes has evolved into journaling, now done habitually at the end of each day and has, on more than one occasion, proven to be more than just CYA activity. Today, I had noted a minor inconsistency between statements given on different dates by a witness to a suspected terrorist activity. Making notes to guide my activities for tomorrow, I reached to answer the phone, "McLean here."

Jeanette Arnold, the secretary to James Olsen, the Chief of Counter-Terrorism Division located at FBI Headquarters in the Hoover Building spoke, "Colt, the boss has made an appointment for you to interview Tennessee Congressman Johnny Mack Davis this afternoon at three o'clock."

"In which of the three buildings is he located?"

"His office is in the Rayburn building, but you are to meet him at his rental property in Great Falls, Virginia. He indicated that his life had been threatened and that several things that he wanted to share with us are located there rather than at the office."

She provided his address on Seneca Road and indicated that she would send directions to my e-mail, then ended the conversation by saying, "He wants to get in some work with his prized Tennessee Walking Horse before it gets dark, so don't be late."

I began to rearrange my plans for the day immediately. First, I decided to pull up the congressman's biographical sketch from the internet and read it while waiting for Jeanette's directions to come in via e-mail. It read: "Johnnie Mack Davis, (born March 15, 1963) is a retired Investment Banker from Nashville, TN. He was first elected as a Democrat representing the 6th Congressional district in 2012. He attributes his election success on his strong stance against Islam.

"Married to Thelma Jane Hardee Davis, from Greenville, North Carolina on June 7, 1992. They have one son Jimmy Alva Davis, born January 26, 1997. Jimmy currently attends Boston College on a full scholarship as a cheerleader.

"Mack, as he prefers to be called, is a self-made millionaire based on his successful investing primarily in the dot-com stocks in the latter part of the twentieth century. He attended Vanderbilt University, receiving a Business Administration Degree in 1985 and an MBA degree in 1987.

"His father and grandfather were farmers in Davidson County and his mother taught school in the Nashville city school system for many years.

"An accomplished horseman, he aspires to enter his horse, General Sherman, in the Tennessee Walking Horse Championship to be held in Shelbyville, TN in either 2018 or 2019, depending upon his legislative schedule.

"He has favored the repeal of the inheritance tax and the marriage tax penalty legislation and has supported the President's ban on Muslim travel to the United States until better vetting procedures can be developed.

"Committee assignments include Energy and Commerce, Banking,Housing and Urban Affairs and Homeland Security.
2240 Rayburn HOB
Washington, DC 20515
T (202) 225-1615
F (202) 225-7998"

I read the bio three times, seeking to memorize as much as possible, and then checked my e-mail for the directions Jeanette had promised. They were there and included a timeline for the drive. It had been quite some time since I had been out that way, but I remembered it as a beautiful, hilly, curvy drive, so I allowed an extra fifteen minutes to make sure I would not be late.

Pulling into the long gravel driveway, at precisely 3 o'clock, I was surprised to find a very modest, small cottage with a nicer barn and riding rink about 100 yards to the rear. The congressman was walking towards the house, still in his business suit, so I assumed that he had just arrived. He stopped, and we exchanged introductions. He invited me in and indicated that I should fix myself a glass of ice tea from the pitcher in the refrigerator, while he changed clothes. I declined the offer but asked instead for permission to use the bathroom; it had been a long drive.

About ten minutes later, he came into the living room, wearing jeans, cowboy boots and a heavy sweater, carrying a glass of tea in one hand and several items in the other. He placed the items on the coffee table in front of him as he sat on the sofa. Even before he began to speak, my mind began to catalog things about him that I would record later that evening. About 55 years of age, impressive physical condition, graying at the temples, tall 6' 2", weight about 240 pounds. An exceptional set of pearly whites, kind eyes that communicated an inward goodness. I liked him immediately.

Clearing his throat, he said, "Colt, Jim Olsen assures me that you are one of his best agents. He spoke to your dedication, and to the fact that you log more hours on the job than any of his other assets. I did some checking of my own as I like to know the people with whom I work. As I understand it, you grew up not too far from here, is that correct?"

"Yes sir, just over on the other side of Clarkes Gap, in the Shenandoah Valley."

He continued with, "You have an impressive military record, and I was pleased to see that as a language expert you are fluent in Arabic. That may serve us both well in the future because I am confident that the threats that were made on my life resulted from my stance against Islam."

He reached down to the materials he had placed on the coffee table and held up a large zip-lock bag turning it so that I could see both sides of the bag. One had a note with large Arabic script that I could easily interpret. The other was the English interpretation which read. Infidel, you are as good as dead. Allah will seek revenge. Count your days. He held up another, somewhat smaller plastic bag which contained the envelope in which the note had been mailed. It was addressed to his office in the Rayburn building and had a postmark indicating that it was sent from Fairfax, Virginia.

He continued with, "I seriously doubt that there is any valuable information in either of these bags since several people in my office had handled them before I was even aware they existed, but I know you guys will give it your best shot."

Next, he pushed a stack of DVD cases toward me saying, "These are videos of speeches I have given over the past several months, in which I am trying to get the American public to wake up to the fact that it is not just the so-called radical Islamist that we should be worried about, but indeed all Islamists. In anticipation that there might be objections or even demonstrations present at some of the speeches, my cameraman had been instructed to scan the audiences often for reactions, rather than just focus on me. Hopefully, you will be able to pick up on something in the videos and use your facial recognition technology to get some leads."

I reached out and picked up the six-DVD cases and made

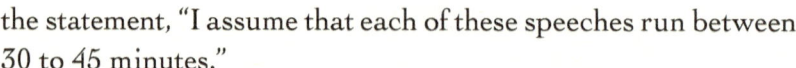
the statement, "I assume that each of these speeches run between 30 to 45 minutes."

"Give or take a minute or two on either end," he responded.

"Well, I can see that I will be burning the midnight oil tonight, but before I rush off, I thought there had been more than one threat."

"There were two phone calls to the office; the first was such a shock that the receptionist did not get the recording device turned on before the caller hung up. The gist of that call was the same as contained in the note. The second call, we believe to be a crank call, you will need to talk to Denise Williamson about that."

I asked for his business card and the telephone numbers here at the house as well as his cell phone number. He reached into his pocket and selected a card from the black leather wallet, taking a pen from the table, he wrote the requested numbers on the back of the card. Noting the business numbers on the front of the card, I took the items he had given me, stood and said, "I know you want to exercise your horse, so I better get on my way."

As we walked toward my car, he said, "Can you take a minute to meet my pride and joy?"

Knowing he meant his horse, and because I am a horse lover, I responded, "I would like that."

With that, he put two fingers up to his mouth and gave a shrill whistle. I heard a neigh come from the back pasture and watched as a magnificent coal black stallion came galloping up to the fence we were approaching. The size, conformation, muscles, bulging veins in his face and neck combined to give the immediate impression, what an athlete! He said, "Colt, meet General Sherman."

The sight of that beautiful animal sticking his head over the fence to be scratched by his master and the deep rumbling sound coming from his throat demonstrated the love between the two; I could only mutter, "Wow!" After extending my hand for him to smell me, I slowly reached up to scratch his forehead and said, "General Sherman, you are special."

"Yes, he is, and my wife often tells people that I love him more than I do her because I bring him to Virginia, where I spend most of my time, while I leave her in Tennessee. I assure you that isn't true, and she knows it because we endure the separation so that my serving in Congress does not interrupt the life of our son."

But, I must ask, "Why the name, General Sherman?"

"A friend of mine, from east Tennessee, raised him, and his family had historically been Union sympathizers. So, that is the name on his registration papers, and I didn't have the heart to change it. Besides, it seems to fit him, I think."

I nodded, extended my hand and said, "Sir, I will contact you as soon as I have anything worthy of your time."

"Thank you, Colt, and please call me Mack, almost everyone does, you know."

Checking to see that there was no traffic behind me at the stop sign, I quickly dialed the Congressman's office and asked to speak with Mrs. Williamson. When she answered, I introduced myself and told her that I was, at Mack's request, investigating the threats made of his life. "I need to come to the office to talk to anyone who knows about the two phone calls in question," I said.

"Oh, Mr. McLean, I have to leave the office by 4:30, my son, Josiah has a game tonight, and I need to fix him a good dinner before we leave, can we do it tomorrow?"

"No problem, let's see how tomorrow works out when it is convenient for me, I will call to check your schedule. It should only take a few minutes anyway. Tell Josiah, I hope he plays well."

"Thank you, it is only a youth league sponsored by our church, but he does enjoy it. I'll be sure and tell him. Hope to see you tomorrow, and God bless you."

I thanked her for the blessing, hung up and headed back to

the office. Arriving at 5:30, I decided to run across the street to my favorite, hole-in-the-wall, Chinese take-out place where I ordered General Tso's chicken, fried rice, one egg roll with a large sweet tea - - to go. Back at the office, I noted that it was 6 PM on the dot, as I began to eat and watch the first DVD.

I watched those DVD's until well after midnight, pausing to study crowd reactions to his remarks – with unsatisfying results I might add. I did mark one scene that was worthy of calling to attention of the facial recognition guys. As dull as it was to watch the same speech over and over, I did have to admit that Mack was passionate about his quest. In every speech he used a common prop which was a copy of the Koran that he had purchased in a local bookstore. He would hold it up for the crowd to see the many red tabs that he had attached. Pointing out that there were well over fifty verses urging Muslims to commit violent acts, such as cutting off the heads and finger-tips of infidels. He always made the point that an infidel was anyone who would not submit to Islam. I noted several quotes that he consistently made:

Chapter 2, verse 216: "Fighting is obligatory for you –"

Chapter 2, verse 193: "Fight against them until idolatry is no more and God's religion reigns supreme."

Chapter 8, verse 12: "I shall cast terror into the hearts of the infidels. Strike off their heads, strike off the very tips of their fingers!"

He ended every speech with these two points: 1. Captured terrorist, when asked why they had committed their acts, always responded, "Because the Koran tells me too." 2. We have let millions of Muslims into our country and they are teaching this crap in their masques every week.

As I drove toward my apartment just south of the Alexandria city limits, I remember thinking, "Well Mack, you just raised the

number of suspects from one to maybe three or four people to over five billion people." As I turned onto Belleview Boulevard the discouraging thought hit me; I still have at least another hour's work to capture the day's events in my journal.

CHAPTER 2

———⟨◆⟩———

OW LONG THE phone had been ringing, I don't know but, I gradually responded to the annoyance, as if I was trying to climb out of a well, opening one eye and reaching for the phone simultaneously --- "Hello," I groaned. The voice of my boss, James Olsen brought me fully awake.

His first words were, "They got him." He went on to say, "Fairfax County police department is on the scene at the Davis place. I have advised the sheriff that we are already involved in investigating threats on his life and that you will be there ASAP. How soon can you get there?"

"I have to hit the shower but will shave on the way, tell them it will be, I did the calculations, about 9:30."

"Okay, come by the office as soon as you have finished out there. I will clear my schedule when you get here. Take some video, I want to see as much as possible, and then we will decide who will take the lead in the murder investigation."

"Yes sir," I said as I jumped out of bed. Sparing you the details, suffice it to say that I made it two minutes ahead of schedule, pulling into the driveway at precisely 9:28 AM. I parked in front of the house, next to Mack's white Prius, and an old Ford pickup truck, I walked toward the back and saw three police cruisers and what I assumed was the coroner's van parked near the barn. Making my way up the slight incline, I noticed

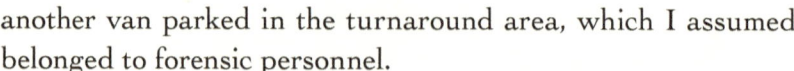

another van parked in the turnaround area, which I assumed belonged to forensic personnel.

In response to the crunching of gravel beneath my feet, the group gathered around parted to give me my first view of Mack's body. To say I was shocked would be the understatement of this young year. These eyes have viewed many horrific death scenes, but the way his body had been positioned on the corral fence as if crucified, brought me to a complete standstill. I gaped in disbelief, and muttered, "What the hell!"

He was dressed in what looked to me to be the same jeans and boots that he had worn yesterday. He also wore a heavy sheepskin lined hoodie which was zipped up to his throat and folded back over the top of the corral post. His legs had been placed through the fence so that his knees were resting on the bottom board of the fence. His hands had been nailed to the top boards, on either side of the post with cement style nails. The hatchet that had apparently been used to drive the nails through his hands lay just to the right of the body. The killer had pulled his shirt out from his pants and had forced a sword, probably a scimitar, up under his rib cage, deep enough to pierce his heart. The handle was facing down toward the ground. Surprisingly, there was very little blood around the body.

After we introduced our selves, I suggested that we each relate what we knew about the event. I started by describing how the FBI Counter Intelligence Division had been called to investigate threats made on the congressman's life, from what he believed was related to his harsh stance on Islam. After relating the information, I had learned yesterday; I asked Mr. Vargas to tell us about what happened this morning.

He began, "My wife Rosa and I live about three miles away, just over in Loudoun County. Mr. Davis rented that place for us when we bring General Sherman here from Tennessee. This place belongs to a friend of his who does not charge him any rent. We left home at exactly 8:15 which probably got us here about 8:20. We went in the front door, using the key he gave us, and when I placed the cookies Rosa had made for Mr. Davis on the kitchen counter, I looked out the kitchen window and saw him nailed to the fence. I rushed out to see if there was anything I could do, but I realized that I should not go to close. Then I rushed back to the house and used the house phone to call 911. The kitchen clock showed it was 8:28. While I was telling what I had seen, Rosa ran to the window; I tried to stop her. She was so upset; I had to hold her from falling. After I hung up, I took her to the couch and asked her to stay there. Then I waited outside until Officer Ellis arrived. Wait, I did go to the barn to try and calm General Sherman, he was very nervous, you see how he spread manure all over the place. But I only touched him, none of his tack or anything else."

Officer Charles "Chuck" Ellis spoke next, saying "I got the call to proceed to this address at about 08:30 as I had just patrolled the Great Falls business section. I was here within five minutes but was so shocked at finding him like this; I did not note the exact time. I started taking pictures with my phone camera and called in to confirm the murder at exactly 8:37. I was advised to wait for Mr. Adams and the crime lab folks and later received another call to let me know that the FBI would also be involved." In between those calls, I interviewed Mr. Vargas, and my notes agree with what he just said."

Fairfax County Coroner, Justin Adams related that he was advised of the murder just as he was preparing to leave his home in Herndon, Virginia for the office. He stated, "I arrived at the scene at 9:02 am. After taking pictures and hearing the reports from Mr. Vargas and Officer Ellis, I climbed down the fence, walking on the bottom board, to the body. He has a nasty bump on the back of his head, with a laceration that had caused blood to seep down his neck. I saw a piece of paper sticking out of the left pocket of his hoodie, so I used tweezers to extract and bag it. Following the fence back to the barn, I was able to see a small blood spot on the cement floor, close to the horse's head. While Mr. Vargas calmed the horse; I was able to obtain a sample, which I feel confident will prove to be that of Congressman Davis." He then held up the small plastic bag which contained a small sheet of paper that looked as if it had been ripped from a spiral binder of some kind. It read, I John 2: 9. He continued, "I Googled it, and it reads 'He that saith he is in the light, and hateth his brother, is in darkness.' So, the question is, did he write this or did the killer or killers leave this as a clue?"

I interjected, "This makes no sense ---"

He replied, "Let me finish. In my opinion, he was secured to the fence by his hoodie, his arms and legs were then placed over the fence boards, and then he was stabbed with the scimitar. I think the weapon pierced his heart and it stopped beating immediately, which explains why there is so little blood on the weapon or the ground. It would have collected in the stomach cavity. I think the killer then went to the tack room to retrieve the equipment used to nail him to the fence. The real puzzle to me is the extreme effort that was used to cover the tracks around the body. Obviously, someone used a small camping type shovel to go deep enough so that it would be impossible to tell what had been obliterated. If a piece of equipment was used to move the body, it must have had two or four wheels. Then a stiff brush was used to sweep the whole area clean. That same procedure was also used on the other side of the driveway, where there is a strange print that was not swept away. I have taken pictures and we will make a cast of it before we leave."

We all walked over to examine the print he spoke of; it looked to me to have been made by a piece of equipment. It measured out at 26 inches wide and two inches in depth, with six well defined screw imprints. There was an imperfection in the form of a small v, almost dead center of the outer edge like a chip had been broken from the metal. We speculated that it was too small to have been left by a scoop, even that of a small bobcat. No one could come up with a good explanation as to what it was.

At that point, I asked Jose, "Can you unsaddle General Sherman, without touching the outside of the saddle, we will need to dust it for prints."

"I can do that, but it is a waste of time," he responded. He quickly added, "I know this horse, as upset as he was no one, other than Mr. Davis or me, would have dared get close enough to touch his saddle."

I watched as he unsaddled, draping the saddle atop the nearest stall, and led the horse into the back stall. I heard him talking to the horse, "Jose will give you a good rub-down, put on your blankie, then I am going to close the doors so that you can get a nice nap. How does that sound to you, big boy?"

I called out, "Jose, is there a shop broom here in the barn?"

"Yes sir, just inside the tack room."

After looking in the tack room thoroughly, I called back, "It is not here."

"No problem, I use the big shovel to scoop the poop."

I realized that he missed the point that the killer(s) probably had taken it.

Justin then directed the two crime scene technicians to, "One of you dust the saddle for prints, and the other get the small whisk broom from my van and see if, by moving some of the loose dirt around, we can uncover any hidden prints."

While they were busy following his orders the rest of us decided to give our opinions about what had happened here. I started out with, "I am about 90 percent sure that this does not involve terrorism, the previous death threat written in Arabic and the use of the scimitar, not-withstanding. If this had been an Islamist, they would have beheaded him.

Officer Ellis, opined "I'm leaning toward there being two or more people involved. That is a big man out there; he must weigh between 235 and 250 pounds. I don't see how even a very

strong man could have gotten him from the barn and upon that post without help."

Coroner Adams offered, "The use of the scimitar, in a thrusting blow, not a swinging motion, certainly supports the theory that an extremely strong person made the attack. To remove his shirt and penetrate through the stomach to get to the heart also indicates some medical knowledge. I also think that he must have known the attacker to have allowed himself to be hit from behind. If it had been a stranger, I doubt he would have turned his back on him."

That was an interesting theory that I had not considered. Then I asked Officer Ellis to call his office to see if the Congressman's family or office had been notified. As he was doing that Jose came out of the barn and headed to the house. He said, "I need to get my Rosa home, this has been very bad for both of us."

I asked him to "Please leave the back door open as we will want to look around the house before we leave. We will lock up." Turning to the others, I said, "The decision as to the FBI's involvement, in this case, is way above my pay grade, but I assume they will want me to dig a little deeper into the terrorist theory. Probably by interviewing Mrs. Davis and some of his associates in the office and in Tennessee. So, let's agree to exchange information until that decision is made."

We exchanged phone and fax numbers, and I told them that I intended to take the Congressman's copy of the Koran with me as evidence and that I would return it to the family after, I had verified the quotes he had been making. I did so, leaving the property at exactly 11:55.

I made it to the Hoover building by 1:35, having stopped in Great Falls for a burger and fries. True to his word the boss called me into his office almost immediately. He showed visible shock as I began to play the video recording of the scene. While I related my activities; he buzzed Jeanette, who stuck her head in immediately. Holding up his hand to indicate I should pause for a minute, he instructed her to "Get a techie to download the latest video from Colt's phone into our system, e-mail me a copy, and get this phone back up ASAP." I continued, emphasizing the fact that I did not see this as an act of terrorism. I finished the briefing with the fact that a decision needed to be made as to which agency would take the lead. He reflected momentarily and then said, "Tell Fairfax County they have the lead but to keep us closely informed as we will continue to be involved. I want you to get down to Tennessee, talk to his wife and pay close attention to his church crowd. Look for any loonies that may be out there. Stay in close touch with me; I have a bad feeling about this one."

At Jeanette's desk, I saw my phone laying there and confirmed that the techies had finished with it before asking her to make the necessary travel arrangements for my Nashville trip. That accomplished, I waited until I was in my car in the parking garage before I dialed Mack's office. Robert Thompson answered on the second ring and advised me that Denise Williamson had been sent home as she was too distraught to work. I explained that I was going to Nashville tomorrow and asked him to notify Mrs. Davis that I would need to ask her a few questions. He gave me the residential number for the Williamson's in Mitchellville, Maryland as well as that of Mrs. Davis in Nashville. Then said, "I will call her right away but please give her a ring when you get into town to arrange a good time to drop in."

After making that agreement and hanging up, I dialed the Maryland number and a male voice answered. "This is Jim, how can I help you."

I identified myself and asked to speak with Denise. There was a long pause before he said, "I really don't want to wake her, I gave her some extra strength Tylenol, and she just dozed off."

"Well Jim I am going to Nashville tomorrow to interview

Mrs. Davis and although I wanted to talk to her about the threatening phone call she took, it can certainly wait. Just have her call me on my cell phone when it is convenient."

He said, "Look I can probably help you with that. She thinks she recognized the voice of a neighborhood boy who has a dislike for our stance for the Lord and has on several occasions delighted in shocking her with foul language. The call was very vulgar, and I'm sure she would not like to relive it. She was convinced that even though he mentioned Mr. Davis's stance against Islam, the intent was to shock her, not to threaten the congressman. I can give you his name if you think it worth checking out, but I know he was in school today and could not have been involved in killing Mr. Davis."

I thanked him and advised that I would get back in touch if I thought it necessary. Just before I hung up, I remembered to ask about Josiah's basketball game.

"They won by just a few points, and he was happy to have gotten more playing time than usual. He was a happy boy!"

The next morning, I arrived at Nashville Airport (BNA) at 11:15 and went straight to the rental car area. After signing the rental contract, I was scanning the city map provided when the pretty young rental agent asked if I needed help. "I'm looking for Curtiswood Lane", I responded.

"Oh, going to the Governor's Mansion, are you?" Before I could respond, she said, "That is easy just take I 40 West, bear left on to I 440, get off at Old Franklin Road, head North toward town, you will turn left onto Curtiswood Lane in just a few blocks. Lots of country music stars use to live in that area, but most of them have either died or moved out to more secluded estates." Then she pointed to the map to show that "Hank Williams, lived there, Porter Wagoner there, Tex Ritter there, Minnie Pearl lived there, and our congressman that was killed yesterday lives about there."

I thanked her and left without explaining why I was

interested in the area. The white Toyota rental was parked right where it was supposed to be, I threw my overnight bag on the back seat and dialed Mrs. Davis's number. Surprised that she answered the phone, I identified myself and asked for a convenient time to stop by. She said, "Now is as good as any, and you can help eat some of this food everyone keeps dropping off. I don't have an appetite so it will be nice if you can help with that."

"I will be there in just a few minutes," I said. The directions I had been given were accurate and easy to follow, so it was indeed only a few minutes before I pulled into the driveway and rang the doorbell. Thelma Jane Davis answered the door, holding out her hand and introducing herself. My first assessment was about 55 years of age, very curly black hair, actually salt, and pepper, beautiful smile, sad eyes. I remember thinking, "I bet she was a knock out when he first met her. What am I thinking, she's no slouch now." I couldn't help but ask, "Don't you have someone here to help with answering the phone and the doorbell?"

"Yes, several of my friends are in the kitchen, but they are chattering away as if nothing had happened, probably trying to me keep me distracted, but frankly, all the chatter is driving me crazy, so I just said, "I'll get it. Come on in, I will ask someone to fix you a plate and bring it to the sunroom, we will have more privacy there."

After telling her about my meeting Mack the day before yesterday and about how I had reviewed recordings of the speeches that he had given me, I asked her, "What information did the Fairfax County Policy provide you as to what happened yesterday?"

She related that they told her that her husband had been killed at the farm that morning and when she pressed for more information they reluctantly admitted that he was stabbed with a scimitar. She immediately started begging me for more details, saying, "I don't understand why, but I have this deep sense that

I need to know more – I feel like I need to know everything he went through before he died."

"Mrs. Davis, even if I were allowed to tell you the things I know and saw, I would not do so, for your own good. I took pictures of the scene, and those have been downloaded to the FBI system and erased from my phone, but the images are in my head, and I wish to God they were not there. I am sure that when we find his killer or killers, and we will find them, things will come out, and you will learn more. Please do not let the details add to your misery and discomfort you are now dealing with. Hopefully, you can take comfort in knowing that he did not suffer. Evidence indicates that he was knocked unconscious and his body moved away from his horse before he was killed."

She leaned her head back against the chair, closed her eyes and was silent for several moments, before she said, "Thank God for that." She then admitted that I was probably right and that she would not bother me with any more details. "Now, let's get on with the reasons for your being here."

We spent the next half an hour going over my questions about his past, whether he had any business or political enemies, etc. She could not think of any situation or of anyone who had ever been upset enough with anything Mack had ever said or done that would lead them to have done this to him.

I made a quick decision about revealing the next bit of information to her, justifying it as a tie-in to my contacting his church contacts. So, I told her about the note we had found in his pocket and then asked, "Is that something your husband would likely have done?"

"No, I would think that highly unlikely. He did carry a notepad in his inside jacket pocket, but that had a flip top cover, and the pages were glued not spiral bound."

For some reason, I told her about how much I had enjoyed seeing the love between Mack and General Sherman and related how impressed I was with that magnificent animal. "Oh my gosh," she exclaimed. "I have to call Jose and Rosa. It will be necessary to sell the horse, I certainly have no need for him, and I know that both Mack and Jose had dreams of entering him in the World Championship event in Shelbyville either this or next year. I know of two individuals who will fight for the right to own that big fellow, but I think I have to offer Jose first choice if he can afford to pay the price. You will not believe what people are willing to pay for an animal with the capabilities of General Sherman. The Vargas' own a small farm out at Leipers Fork, and I suspect they will want to return now that Mack doesn't need them up there."

I just sat there listening, until she realized what was happening and apologized by saying, "Oh please forgive me, I just realized that I am rambling on about things you aren't interested in."

"No, that is not the case at all. I will be interested in knowing what the future holds for General Sherman."

One final question before I leave, "Who do you think knew the most about Mack's political and religious activities?"

"That's easy; politically it would be his office manager Robert Thompson, and on the religious side it could be our pastor, Rusty Trotter but no I think it would definitely be Gene Wilson, who is a Deacon at our church, Grassland Heights Baptist. The two of them go way back."

I thanked her for her kindness, her time and generosity, commenting on how good the food was and went to the rental car where I dialed the number she had given me for the church. When the receptionist answered, I asked if Pastor Trotter or Mr. Wilson could spare a few minutes to meet with me this afternoon or tomorrow morning. She replied that the pastor's schedule is pretty much booked but asked me to wait while she checked with Gene. Almost immediately, she back on the line and said, "He said to tell you to come on."

Using directions given to me by Mrs. Davis, I followed

my tracks back to Franklin Road and headed south toward Brentwood. I pulled into the church parking lot about fifteen minutes later. Mr. Wilson met me in the church foyer, and after our introductions, he said: "Come on back to the family center, I have coffee brewing, and there is no one else around, you can help me finish off the pot."

As we walked toward the back of the building, I remarked about being lucky enough to catch him on such short notice and expressed the hope that I could finish up in time to change my flight to this evening rather than tomorrow afternoon. He replied, "No luck involved in finding me here, even though I am not on the staff, I do spend a great deal of my time here – I try to help wherever I can." With that said, he reached for two mugs and filled them with coffee and went over to a table where he placed a cup and invited me to sit.

As soon as I told him that I had just left the Davis residence, he interjected, with a question, "How is Thelma Jane doing today?"

"As well as can be expected," I said.

"The pastor and I spent several hours there yesterday; she really took it hard even though she had thought many times that something like this could happen. Since the FBI is involved, may I assume that terrorism is suspected?"

"Not necessarily so, we are involved because we were looking into threats on his life that he was convinced happened due to his stance against Islam. Frankly, I think that we are just as likely to find someone who is unstable due to political or religious, other than Islamic, views. So, how about you telling me what you know about Mack and anything that you can recall about those who might have had differences or difficulties with him in the past." With that, I placed the small recorder on the table, switched it to the on position and sat back and took my first sip of coffee.

He took a swig of coffee, sat the cup on the table, brought

his hands up toward his chin, started tapping the fingers of each hand together, and there was a significant pause as he evidently contemplated how he wanted to proceed. "We were classmates in high school, graduated from West End High School, just up the road, played baseball together for three years. Unfortunately, for us, those were not the glory days for West End baseball. Bob Greene, the best pitcher to ever come out of these parts, had graduated a few years before us, so we struggled through losing seasons. Lost touch with each other for several years but eventually, we both wound up in the banking business, but with different companies. So, we could reminisce, talk about investments, that sort of thing and we were certainly friends, but not close friends. Our political views kept us from being too close. I would describe Mack as a centrist democrat while I am about as far right on the political spectrum as you can get. My personal view is that we have allowed the government to consume far too much or many of our resources as is wise." He paused, and then said, "As for identifying people who had difficulties with him, I can only think of one. There is a local State Senator, a Republican, they have taken verbal shots at each other in the past, but I know for a fact, he has been here for Senate sessions all week. I'm sure there are some who would disagree with him on his stance against Islam, I am not one of those, but I can't think of anyone who would want to harm him. The worst thing I can think of that anyone ever said about him, was 'He is more liberal with other people's money than he is with his own.' But, shoot that could be said about any liberal."

We quickly wrapped things up, said our goodbyes and I was able to change my flight, cancel my hotel reservations, and head home.

CHAPTER 3

FRIDAY MORNING, I reached the office feeling refreshed for the first time in days and began using my journal to put the events of the previous few days into an acceptable FBI report format. I noted the fact that I had checked all of the quotes Mack had used in his speeches and had confirmed that he had accurately quoted the Koran. I then reviewed the official coroner's report that Dr. Adams had faxed to me. There were no surprises therein. It did confirm the time of death, the fact that the scimitar had indeed pierced the heart and that there were no fingerprints, other than Mack's on the saddle, and that no prints were found on the note. A couple of phone calls back and forth to the Fairfax County Police Department completed the sharing of information and left both sides thinking the best lead we had was the unusual track found on the other side of the driveway. At one o'clock I forwarded the report to headquarters and went to Arby's for my favorite fast food sandwich, their Smokehouse Bacon Brisket, curly fries, and a Pepsi. While I enjoyed my lunch, I basked in the sunlight reflecting through the plate glass window and ponder the things that I had pending back at the office. By four o'clock, I had finished my cleanup tasks, so I called Jeanette Arnold to find out if the boss had seen my report. She indicated that "He reviewed it as soon as it arrived if he hasn't called you by now, I doubt that you will hear from him today. Why don't you call it a day, you have had a busy week?"

I took her advice, left the office and proceeded to the dry cleaners to pick up my suits and shirts and on to Golden China for carry-out. Settling back in my recliner, I thought. "Ah the life of 40-year-old sex symbol, working crossword and sudoku puzzles, eating out of cardboard boxes, watching Blue Bloods and thinking ahead to watching college basketball all day Saturday. Surely, it can and hopefully will, get better than this."

My plan to sleep late was derailed at 8:05 with the shrill ringing of my land line. It was Jim Olsen. "We have another congressman down," was his first words.

I stammered out, "Who?"

"The Beaufort County, North Carolina Sheriff's Department was called to the residence of Congressman Herbert Connor early this morning in response to a 911 call from a neighbor. A deputy found the congressman amid the rubble of a cinder block wall that surrounds the swimming pool. I don't like this, two congressmen killed within days of each other gives me really bad vibes. I think our travel budget can afford a couple of nights hotel bill and gas money; I want to know if the two cases are related in any way. Are you willing to take on the job?"

"Yes sir, I was involved in a case down there a few years back involving a young deputy sheriff in that department, and it will be nice to renew those acquaintances. I'll get on the road as soon as I can, I should be back in the office Monday morning and will get you a report as early as I can."

I dressed and packed for a two-day stay as fast as I could, then thought to pull up a biography from the same site I had visited a few days earlier. The info I wanted came up with just a few clicks of the mouse:

"Herbert Charles Conner, born August 28, 1947, in Aurora, North Carolina. Married to his high school sweetheart, Sally Ann Clark, June 22, 1970. They have three daughters, all of whom are married and he and Sally Ann are the proud grandparents of six grandchildren (four girls and two boys).

"Herbert received his Political Science degree from North Carolina State University in 1969. He took over the management of his family farm that same year.

"His political career began in 1975 when he was elected to the Board of Commissioners where he served until 1980. He was then elected to the North Carolina State Senate where he served ten years. In 1990 he was elected to the United States House of Representatives and has served consecutive terms since then. He is currently the ranking member of the Committee on Resources (formerly the Merchant Marine and Fisheries Committee) where is an avid supporter of all marine and fishery issues. He serves on the Board of Directors of the Aurora Fossil Museum, a natural science museum established in 1976.

"Herbert is proud of his record of working with his colleagues from across the aisle to achieve results that have benefitted the people of Eastern North Carolina.

400 Cannon Office Building
Washington, DC 20515
T (202) 225-3303
F (202) 225-3553"

An hour later, I was cruising down I 95 south thinking about how nice it would be to see Brody Edwards again. What an amazing few days that had been, I can hardly believe that nearly four years have passed since I was involved in trying to protect Brody from a terrorist determined to take revenge on him. Brody had wounded the man, a member of the Taliban, in Afghanistan, had been credited with killing many of his friends and a year later when the President turned down the Marine Corps recommendation for rewarding Brody with the Congressional Medal of Honor, Brody's identity became national news. The terrorist came to America determined to behead Brody. In what I thought was the most amazing set of circumstances, all of which Brody claimed was the hand of God at work, Brody arrived at Dulles Airport, to pick up someone, at the same time the terrorist got into a waiting car. Following that car to a nearby mosque, led to an inside CIA informant determining that the man's purpose was to kill Brody. The CIA planned to capture the terrorist when he left the mosque, but the terrorist evaded that trap. A new plan was quickly put together where the FBI joined the CIA and the Beaufort County Sheriff's office in setting a new trap in Brody's home territory. The ensuing weird circumstances (my words) or miraculous events (Brody's words) would make a great movie ending. Using a string of firecracker explosions as well as that of a misfiring motorcycle to distract our attention away from Brody, the terrorist, using scuba equipment, arose from the creek, knocked Brody unconscious, took him underwater to a nearby boat and was across the river before we knew what happened. Brody was handcuffed, with his own cuffs and taken to his church where the intended killer meant to behead him and leave his corpse at the church door. The event that reversed the situation, putting Brody in charge and the terrorist in cuffs could only be described as miraculous even by nonbelievers, but since Brody had declared his intention to write a book about it all, I will leave that story for him to tell.

I arrived in Washington just after 3:30 and decided to go to the Sheriff's office first. Opening the door, I was greeted with the view of Ellen Buck, AKA Right Arm bent over looking in the credenza behind her desk. At the next instant, I hear Brody call out, "Where is my file on the Matthews case?"

"You left it on top of the filing cabinet for me to put away, as usual," she replied.

At that point, even though I was enjoying the view, I cleared my throat to get her attention. She obviously realized the awkwardness of her position because she was blushing when she stood erect, turned toward me and said, "Well I'll be, it's the FBI, what are doing down here Agent McLean?" Before I could answer, she called out, "Hey Donnie and Brody, get out here, we have company."

In the next thirty minutes, we updated each other on what had transpired since we last met. I learned that Donnie was now Sheriff Gurganus, that Brody was now Sergeant Edwards and that he and Barbara Jean had twins, soon to be four years old, with another baby due in a few weeks. Ellen said, "I am still waiting for Prince Charming." I admitted to being a workaholic and to having no social life. That was when Brody said, "Hey maybe you two should get together, with social media the way it is; it's a lot easier to carry on a long-range courtship that it once was." Neither of us responded to his remark, but it was obvious that we were contemplating it, just not ready to verbalize our thoughts.

To cover the awkwardness of the moment, I said, "It is about time we get down to business. I am here to look into the death or your congressman, really to see if there is any connection to the death of Congressman Davis which happened in Fairfax County three days ago."

The four of us went down the hall to the conference room, Ellen remained standing in the doorway so as to see the front door, while the three of us sat down and Brody began the briefing. "The 911 call came in at 7: 35 this morning from a Mike Richmond, a neighbor, and friend, who drove past and saw that the privacy fence for the back-yard pool was down. He was on his way to meet his pals for coffee, not wanting to be late, and knowing that Mrs. Connor and her daughter were in New York, he called in and asked us to check it out. Our closest asset was summoned and he arrived about fifteen minutes later to find not only had the wall been deliberately pulled down but that the congressman, in his PJ's and bathrobe was dead. Based on his body temperature, the coroner estimated the time of death to be between midnight and one AM. Our best guess as to what happened is that someone drove in and opened the double iron gate to the backyard and backed a vehicle, probably a truck all the way to the pool house area, threw a grappling hook over the wall, secured by a chain or large rope, attached that to the bumper and pulled the wall down. There is burnt rubber on the driveway to back up that theory. We think the Congressman responded to the noise and came out of the house with a pistol. We found the pistol, it is registered in his name, about 20 yards from the body with one spent shell and five live rounds in the chamber. Oddly enough, Mr. Connor was not shot, he was choked to death. We think by someone whom he knew, and then the killer used the gun to shoot out the night light to keep anyone from seeing the body until daylight. We found this note sticking out of his bathrobe pocket," with that said, Brody held up a plastic bag containing the note. I could see the words, Joshua 6: 20. Brody then said, "The Bible verse reads, ...the wall fell down flat."

I then briefed them about Mack's death concluding with the fact that in my opinion there is a definite connection between the two. "I am sure we will find that the notes were from the same notebook and have the same handwriting. The use of bible verses also indicates the same killer. I will also need to view the crime scene, but that will best be done tomorrow in better daylight."

As we all stood, Brody said, "Hey guys, I went fishing yesterday afternoon and caught a large string of rockfish. Barbara Jean is doing a huge pot of stew, with onions, potatoes, carrots and her famous home-made cornbread, why don't the three of you join us and the Cooke's for dinner?"

Donnie quickly opted out saying, "I can't, I promised Mary Ellen, I would take her to Parker's for barbeque tonight."

I looked at Ellen and saw her nodding affirmatively and said, "Sounds good to me." On the way to the front, we agreed that I would pick her up at 5:45. She provided me her address and phone number, in case I got lost, and I went to check in at the motel. Which allowed me just enough time to put away my stuff and clean up. After shaving, I dabbed on a small dash of cologne, which I seldom use, thinking, maybe I will get close enough for her to know I smell good.

On the way to her house, I thought, "Wonder why I didn't notice how pretty she is, the last time I was here?" Then I remembered that Grace had been gone less than a year at that time. I tried to pull up Grace's image, and it was difficult to do so, and I found that disturbing. However, the picture of Ellen kept popping into my brain. Probably about 35 years old, blond hair, always in a ponytail, hazel eyes with flecks of gold, five feet five or so, about 130 pounds all packed into a very feminine figure. She wears a little powder probably to cover a few freckles, maybe a little bit of rouge, but no lipstick. A smile that radiates goodness, I liked that image.

We arrived at the Edwards residence in Chocowinity two minutes before six o'clock. Ellen said, "Pull in the driveway and around the back, that where everyone parks." Inside Brody introduced me to Joe Cooke, the Washington High School baseball coach and his wife, Tilly. Barbara Jean came over to shake my hand and say, "It's good to see you again Colt and under better circumstances than the last time we saw each other." I agreed with that and watched in amusement as four-year-old twins charged into the room. Brody said, "FBI Special Agent Colt McLean I would like you to meet my twins. This is Joseph James, who prefers to be called JJ and this is Hannah Jean, who is not fond of being called HJ, which we sometimes forget and do anyway." JJ stepped forward and gave me a manly handshake while Hannah went to Ellen, who picked her up, giving her a big hug and a kiss on the cheek. Hannah said to Ellen, "Is he your boyfriend?"

"Not my boyfriend but he is a friend of your daddy and Sheriff Gurganus. He did give me a ride here tonight, so I think he is kind of nice, don't you?"

She looked very serious and then said, "He is really big and good looking, maybe you should let him be your boyfriend."

I chimed in with, "What a little charmer you are. Ellen and I will talk about that and let you know what we decide." Ellen put her down, and they were both off like a whirlwind.

The next three hours seemed to fly by, the meal was delicious, the company was delightful, and I remember thinking, I haven't had this much fun in years. Being around a loving family and people who apparently were best of friends was just what I needed. I felt rejuvenated and alive for the first time in ages. I could not keep my eyes off Ellen, and I caught her blushing on several occasions as she caught me staring. I was able to make arrangements with Brody to have him take me to the Connor residence tomorrow morning for a look see. I quickly added, "I promise we will be back in time for you to go to church."

As we were saying goodbye and thank you for the meal and lovely evening, Brody handed me a book entitled Beneath the Shadow of the Cross. This is the story I wrote about my service in the Marines, my injury and encounter with the terrorist plot that you were involved in. I signed the inside cover. Hope you enjoy it." I admired the front cover showing a beautiful country church with the shadow of the cross on the front lawn, flipped to the inside cover to see his inscription, thanked him and offered to pay him for the book. "Oh no, I have given copies to everyone involved in the story, you just tell your friends about it, maybe that will generate some interest and help the sales," he said. "It is available at Amazon.com in both the paperback, like you have, as well as in e-book format."

Driving back to her house, I said to Ellen, "I don't know that I have ever laughed as much as I did tonight."

"It was fun, wasn't it," she replied. "I couldn't help but laugh when BJ referred to herself as 'AKA the Blimp.'"

"How about when she said, 'I just waddled right out of there', now that was funny."

As we parked in front of her house on 2ⁿᵈ street, I left the car running with the heater on high turned to Ellen and said, "I need to tell you that I am highly in favor of Brody's suggestion that 'Maybe you two should get together.' In fact, my thoughts have been toying with the idea throughout the evening."

"Really, well I must confess that I have tossed the idea around a time or two as well. The problem, in addition to the long-distance part of it, is that I can more easily see you as Prince Charming that I can see myself as a damsel in distress."

"Oh, I beg to differ, I see you having been captured in the position of taking care of your ailing aunt for years, as being Right Arm at work, the only one who can keep the ship on course, so to speak. It makes me want to ride to the rescue, place you on a pedestal, and show you the beauty and synergism involved in progressing toward two becoming one." I was astonished to see tears begin to flow down her cheeks and I quickly added, "Am I moving too fast here?"

"Oh no, not at all, I am just reacting to the music of my heartstrings, that may be the most beautiful beginning I can imagine to any courtship. Now take me to the front door and let's get this relationship rolling with our first kiss."

One the front porch, I turned on my phone to provide light for her to see the keyhole and then we embraced. We stood there for what seemed like a long time before I said, "This would be even nicer if we didn't have on these heavy coats."

"There is no law that says you can't hold me tighter," she said. And so, I did. The kiss that followed will forever be etched in my memory; it was so sweet. I do remember telling her, "You taste, smell and feel so good to me."

I explained what I had to do tomorrow morning with Brody and then suggested that I could pick her up by 10:30 and we could go to church and have lunch before I have to drive back to Virginia. She like that and we ended the night with a short peck of a kiss on the lips.

Back at the motel, I had to force myself to journal the events of the day, rather than read Brody's story, but as it turned out, I did have time to do both. I actually read the first four chapters before cutting off the light at midnight.

On Sunday morning I picked up Brody at exactly 8:30 as we had agreed to and we proceeded down 33 East to the Connor residence. I pulled into the driveway and parked behind a red Cadillac Escalade, which I assumed to belong to Mrs. Connor. We walked toward the backyard, ducked down under the crime scene tape and Brody pointed out where the pistol had been found. I noted the glass from the night light had not been cleaned up and listened carefully as he showed me the burnt rubber marks on the pavement and where the body had been placed. I estimated that a section of about six feet of the wall had been pulled down. Only the bottom row of cinder block had remained in place. There were scratches and indentations of the top block to confirm the theory that a grappling hook-like device had been used to bring the wall down. As we walked back toward the house, I noted a place just in front of the rubber marks where there was no grass. Looking at the small rounded bare spot, I saw a slight imprint, similar to that I had seen at the Davis property. We both took pictures of it with our phones and decided that the print was too shallow and small to warrant trying to make a cast of it. I had just told Brody that I would send him a picture of the larger print we had taken at the Davis crime scene when Mrs. Connor came out the back door.

Brody introduced us explaining to her that I was here to see if there is any possible connection between this and the death of Tennessee Congressman Davis a few days ago in Virginia. She reacted immediately by saying, "And do you see any?"

"Yes ma'am, there are some, and I would like to talk to you about them if we can go inside out of this cold."

She invited us in and offered us coffee, which we both gratefully accepted. I explained the similarity of a bible verse citation having been left at both scenes and asked Brody to show her a picture of the note they had found in her husband's bathrobe pocket, and he did so. She responded to my question, "That is definitely not Herbert's handwriting."

I went on to explain that the bodies of both men were posed as if the killer or killers were trying to convey a message. "A message which I am sorry to say we simply do not understand."

She began to cry, saying "I certainly don't understand it. Why would anyone want to hurt Herbert, he has served for over twenty years without a hint of any scandal. Why I would bet my last dollar that he has more friends on both sides of the aisle than any other congressman in Washington. In fact, I am convinced the very reason that he gets reelected in this largely Republican based district is that he tries to work with the other party to get things done that are best for all of us. That is what people really want, not this my way or the highway attitude that seems to prevail." She paused to wipe her eyes, and I remained silent allowing her to collect her thoughts. Finally, she began again, "It has to be because he supports the President's policy to control access to our country and to build the wall. Nothing else makes sense to me, at the bottom of his murder you will likely find a disgruntled democrat who doesn't want to see us working together for the common good. It is so sad that people are so set on having their own way that they cannot see the value of other views. I just hate this divisiveness!"

I thanked her for her time, gave her my business card and asked her to call me if she later thought of anything that might help us in the investigation. On the way back Brody said, "I don't know what political affiliation of the killer will have, but I do agree with Mrs. Connor that the reason for his death has to be because he supported the new president."

Back at Brody's house, we said our goodbyes, and I let him know that Ellen and I had agreed to give his suggestion of

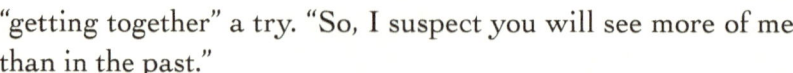
"getting together" a try. "So, I suspect you will see more of me than in the past."

"I would hope so; I don't think a relationship can survive on a four-year hiatus."

I thanked him again for the gift of the book and promised to tell my contacts about how to get a copy. Waving to him and BJ who had stepped out to the front porch, I turned and headed into town.

Walking up the front walkway, I could see Ellen's shadow and knew she was waiting for me, that caused a tingle to run up my spine. After I knocked, she opened the door, and she said, "Get in here Prince." As soon as the door closed she was in my arms, wearing no heavy coat, I might add. I stood there gently rubbing her back, enjoying the smell and feel of her and was finally able to say, "This is a much better way to start the day than reviewing a crime scene."

"I could get used to it," she said.

The drive to Fellowship Bible Church took less than 5 minutes. After parking on the East side lot and while walking toward the front of the church, I nudged her hand with my pinky thinking it would be nice to hold her hand. She said, "Keep your hands to yourself, sir."

"What the heck, are we breaking up already?"

"No, I'm just not ready to give up my reputation as the only 35-year-old virgin in town."

Can you imagine, walking into church with that thought on your mind?

Inside, she introduced me to the man and woman who were assigned to greet people, but I do not remember their names. In the auditorium, I found nicely cushioned chairs, rather than pews. They were arranged in six different sections giving the overall appearance of warmth and comfort. Ellen pointed to the front middle section and said, "I usually sit in that area, is it okay with you?" I nodded, and she let the way to two empty chairs next to the right aisle. When we stood for the first song, I was astonished by the beauty of the voices of a couple sitting two chairs over on the row behind us. They both had their eyes closed and hands in the air lost in worship. I stopped singing so I could hear them better. When we sat, Ellen removed the sermon note page from her bulletin, flipped it over and wrote this note on the back. That is Lashawn and Laverna Johnson, you will read about their beautiful love story in Brody's book. I will introduce you after church is over.

After the service ended, Ellen introduced us telling them about my involvement in Brody's rescue four years earlier. Lashawn said, "I knew I had seen you somewhere before but had been unable to place where. We are grateful for your help; Brody is a friend of ours."

In response to my complimenting them both on the beauty of their voices they gave God praise for the gift they had received. "We do love to sing and try our best to use that gift, as well as our very lives, for His glory," was the way Laverna expressed it.

In the car, we discussed what to do with the short time we had before I had to leave and decided on taking home fast food using the time to get to know each other better. We made it back to her place with a taco salad for her and a burrito and tacos for me. In the kitchen, she poured us each a large glass of sweet tea, and as I started unwrapping my food, she said, "Let's pray." I nodded agreement, and she thanked the Lord for the food and asked Him to bless us both as we work on our relationship with each other. I was deeply touched when she prayed, "Lord, please protect Colt as he goes about his important job of keeping us all safe and help him bring these killings to an end as soon as possible." I echoed her amen.

I won't bore you with details, but I covered growing up on a farm, actually an apple orchard, graduating from Berryville High School, joining the army, losing my parents in the house fire, going to college on the GI Bill, meeting my girlfriend Grace, whom I later married, my time at the FBI Academy, Grace's death in the automobile accident on the beltway, my turning away from God as a result, and my gradual return to the Lord mostly because of Brody's dealing with his life-threatening situation. All this took about an hour, and I ended up by telling her that I had loved my wife but confessed to having some guilt that I had not loved her as deeply as I should have. "Whether due to immaturity or pride in my work, I don't know, but I do want you to know that I am now certain that if I ever have another wife she will have first place in everything I think and do."

I listened carefully as she began to tell her story, how she was born here in Washington, spent her entire life here and was essentially happy, but also had a sense that she had missed out on something important. Her parents had both been school teachers; she was an only child. Her parents were killed in a boating accident on the Pamlico river when she was only 16. How she was spared being in the accident by a last-minute decision to go to the movies with her girlfriends. Her two-year study at the local junior college, how she enjoyed being called Right Arm because it conveyed how much she was needed and appreciated. She related that there had been only one love interest in her life and that had been her senior year in high school. That had ended rather abruptly when he reacted badly to a family situation and joined the air force. "I haven't seen him since," she said. She concluded with the fact that her aunt had left her this house, it is paid for, she had an investment account due to the sale of her parent's house and with the insurance money left after their funeral expenses. She finished by admitted to being inexperienced in relationships and undoubtedly naïve by today's standards, maybe even a little needy - - but, "I am so ready for Prince Charming."

We walked from the kitchen to the sunroom, and she pointed out the huge grape vine that took up most of the backyard, saying, "I love to take a bowl of water out there in the summertime, pick grapes and sit in that Adirondack chair washing and eating scuppernongs until I am full." I learned that another favorite thing for her to do was sit on the front porch swing and chat with neighbor's as they strolled by. We walked through the dining room, which was furnished beautifully, with a set that had to qualify as antique. She opened the laundry room door, I peeked in and noted a stack of plain white undies on the top of the dryer, I commented, "You need to start thinking more about visual impact than about comfort." She apparently knew what I was referring to because she blushed but smiled.

A long goodbye kiss left us both breathing heavily but with a glow of happiness on our faces. We both had our arms around the other's waist, as we leaned back to enjoy the satisfaction we each felt. I mentally checked the fact that I had her phone and e-mail info, and then said, "I think we got this getting together thing off to a good start, don't you?"

"Oh yes, yes I do. Your audition for the role of Prince Charming was very convincing; you have the lead role. Now let's see how you perform."

As I drove away, I was grinning from ear to ear.

CHAPTER 4

MONDAY MORNING, I left my office in Crystal City in time to be at headquarters by 10 AM as prearranged. Upon entering the boss's suite of office's, I knew something was amiss when Jeanette stood up and said, "Go on in, he is waiting for you." Sure enough, the first words out of Jim Olsen's mouth were, "We've got another one."

I'm not sure whether I said or just thought, "Oh no, we have a serial killer on our hands." I know for sure that I asked him, "What do we have?"

"Metropolitan Police, in response to a call from California Congressman Antonio Alvarez's office entered his apartment in Georgetown at 9:38 this morning. They found his body on the living room floor. Their assessment was that he had been dead for hours. That is all we know; you need to get over there and find out what happened. Don't bother to call in just get back here and brief me as soon as you can. This is going to activate all of the big hitters in this town. I'm sure the pressure will demand we take the lead role now." He looked down at a paper on his desk, scribbled the congressman's address on a notepad, tore it off, handed it to me and pointed to the door.

I showed my credentials to the policeman at the apartment door, he handed me a set of booties and a pair of latex gloves from boxes on the floor and opened the door for me. I was somewhat surprised to find the Chief of the Metropolitan Police Force,

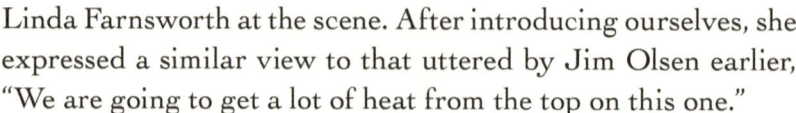

Linda Farnsworth at the scene. After introducing ourselves, she expressed a similar view to that uttered by Jim Olsen earlier, "We are going to get a lot of heat from the top on this one."

I agreed and asked to be briefed on what they have so far.

"We responded to a call from his office, that he was overdue. We were advised that his Chief of Staff, who had the only spare key to the apartment was home for the weekend and not expected back until late afternoon, so after we got no response to our knocks, we picked the lock. Based on body temperature we estimated the time of death to be about five PM yesterday." She walked over to the sheet draped body to pull it back so that I could see, and said, "He was hit in the back of the head, with such force as to completely crush his skull. The coroner thinks he died instantly. There are lots of prints to be gone through; we did see several clots of dirt in the foyer that looked like they came from the treads of work boots or running shoes. Unfortunately, in the bagging process, they crumbled into dust. I don't think we will get any useful information from that. The best clue we have is this note found on the floor by his body." She held up a plastic bag with the now familiar sized sheet with the words Joshua Chapter 20 printed on it.

I then advised her of the fact that the other two congressmen had specific Bible verses on what appears to be pages from the same notebook, giving her details of each case that had not yet become public knowledge.

She continued by saying, "I took the task of advising his staff of his death." She thumbed through a small notebook and continued, "I talked to his Legislative Assistant Brian Nunez and here is a quote from that conversation, 'It has to be because of the stance he has taken against sanctuary cities'."

I asked several questions about whether there had been any signs of a search having been done or if anything seemed to be out of place or missing.

She said, "No not that we can tell."

Writing down the congressman's office number she gave me, I thanked her and said, "I am sure we will be talking again soon."

On the way to the car, I dialed the number, and Mr. Nunez answered. I asked, "If he had evidence to back up the theory you expressed to Ms. Farnsworth."

"Yes, I have several DVD's of speeches he has given castigating politicians who advocate giving sanctuary to anyone who has broken the law."

"I need to take those as evidence, I will return them to you as soon as we can make copies," I said. He agreed to bag them up and have them at the guard desk by the time I could reach the Longworth House Office Building. I picked them up, grabbed a hot dog and soda from the closest street vendor and was in Jim's office just before 2 o'clock.

I placed the DVD's on Jeanette's desk and asked her to "Have the lab guys burn a copy, place it in a new file entitled Antonio Alvarez and tell them to get it up and running so the boss can review it as soon as he can. I also need the originals and the copy back here PDQ." She nodded and said, "Go on in, just knock, he is waiting."

In response to my knock, I heard, "Come."

That short command conveyed to me that he was feeling the stress. I knew that assessment was correct when he said.

"I was called up to the Chief's office and directed to set up a task force to oversee the resolution of these murders. You will take the lead, and I will dedicate all the resources you need. Now, tell me what you know about the latest case."

While I was bringing him up to speed, I heard my cell phone beep, indicating that a text message had come in, but I did not take time to look at it. "I am going to set up a conference call scheduled every morning at 09:30 between us and all police jurisdictions that are involved, so far that is just three, and hopefully there won't be any more. We need to take a close look at all Congressional Staff, the victims had to have known their assailants to have let them get close enough to hit them in the head. We will look for anyone who is physically strong enough to lift 240 pounds, has enough of a religious background to be able to quote scripture and who might have had personal dealings with any of the deceased. Also, we need to monitor media news, especially those where the public can call in to express opinions. We will look for snarky comments about any of the deceased, or even those of any elected official and get those phone numbers for follow up purposes."

He pulled out his staff directory and said, "Let's look at assets that can be assigned to help you."

I replied, "Let's start with clerical and technical support, rather than agents. I want three, the best we have, one to do the staff check, and one each to monitor radio and television media. Then I identified two agents that I wanted to be available when there is a need. We just do not have enough leads to justify people sitting around with nothing to do."

He seemed to like the direction I was giving, expressed his thanks and said, "Go get em, tiger."

I thanked Jeanette for her help, picked up the DVD's and headed to the garage. In my car, I pulled out my phone to retrieve the text message. It was from Ellen and read, heard the news, know you are busy. Praying for you. I closed my eyes, pushed my head back on the rest and thought how good it felt to have someone doing that. I thanked the Lord and sought His protection and guidance in the days ahead. I asked for a blessing on Ellen as well. With that accomplished, I sent a quick reply that simply said, "Thanks so much, will call later." Then I dialed Mr. Nunez to advise that I would be dropping the CD's at the guard desk in just a few minutes.

Back at the office, I instructed the pool of clerical staff, serving all agents at our location, what needed doing in setting up the conference call each workday morning at 09:30. "Make sure each jurisdiction has my cell phone number for contacts on other than work days," I said. Then I announced my new assignment as head of the Task Force investigating killing members of Congress. With that accomplished, I proceeded to my cubicle to ponder my next moves. It is now 5 P.M, the staff will be leaving, rush hour traffic will be a problem, might as well eat here, I thought. I picked up the phone and dialed, from memory, Domino's Pizza and order my usual small pizza with pepperoni and a large Pepsi. Then called down to the guard desk to clear the delivery boy to come up and went online to pull up the Alvarez biography from the now familiar site.

"Antonio Juan Alvarez, born December 11, 1968, Graduated from Golden Gate University in 1991 with degrees in Computer Science and Political Science. He then went on to Georgetown University where he received his law degree magna cum laude.

"Antonio joined the United States Air Force in 1993 as a member of the JAG Corps. While stationed at Ramstein Air Force Base in Germany, he met a fellow officer who was a nurse at the base hospital. They married at the base chapel two months after their first meeting. He and Maria Chan Alvarez now have two sons, Jonathan and Robert.

"Leaving active duty in 1998, he joined the San Francisco law firm of Carson, Wells, and Hopper where he worked until his election to the United States House of Representatives in 2014.

"His political career began in 2002 when he was elected to the San Francisco City Council. In 2005 he was elected to the State Assembly, and in 2011 he became a California State Senator.

"Antonio is still active in the Air Force Reserves and currently serves as a Colonel stationed at Travis Air Force Base.

"As one of the few computer science majors serving in Congress, he is frequently sought out for his insight on technology including cybersecurity, cloud computing, and innovation.

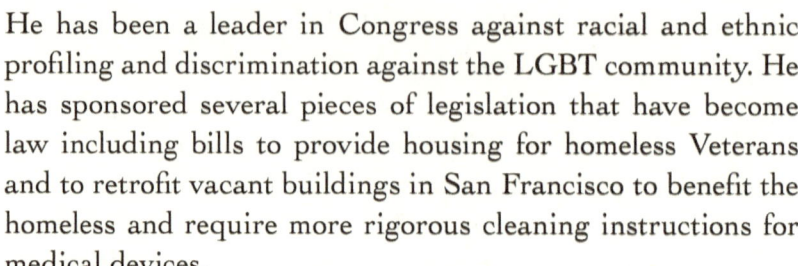

He has been a leader in Congress against racial and ethnic profiling and discrimination against the LGBT community. He has sponsored several pieces of legislation that have become law including bills to provide housing for homeless Veterans and to retrofit vacant buildings in San Francisco to benefit the homeless and require more rigorous cleaning instructions for medical devices.

"He currently serves on the House Judiciary Committee and the Committee on Science and Technology.

3300 Longworth HOB

Washington DC, 205

T (202) 225-6866

F (202) 228-8384"

I read the bio several times as is my custom and then selected the first DVD I had received from Nunez and popped it into my laptop.

It is now 6:30 and I have finished eating and listening to the first DVD. I looked around my work area and thought, "I need a picture of Ellen to go right there." With that, I swiveled back, put my feet up on the desk and dialed her home phone.

"It's Prince Charming," she said answering on the first ring. "I was sitting here debating on how long I could wait to hear from you. How are you?"

"Better now that I hear your sweet voice," I replied. Then I told her about my having the lead role in the Task Force ordered by the Director of the FBI.

"Congratulations," she said. "I guess that will keep you on your toes, and unfortunately maybe even away from me."

"It will undoubtedly make it more challenging to keep my commitment to giving you first place in my life, but I am going to do my best. I plan on coming down Saturday morning, early, and leaving after church on Sunday. Assuming you want me to come?" I added.

"Oh, yes, that sounds good, I will ask Brody if you can use his spare bedroom to save the expense of the motel bill."

"I can afford a night's stay in the motel," was my reply.

"I know, but he will want you to stay there because he has something he wants to discuss with you. Don't make reservations until I check back with him, please."

I agreed, and we talked until I insisted that I had to get my journaling done. "It has become such a habit that my mind will not slow down until it is done. Then I can start planning the next day," I said. Like teenagers, we sent kissing sounds to each other and reluctantly said, "Good night."

Tuesday, February 13th: Kathy a member of the clerical pool stuck her head in and said, "When you hear the beep, pick up for your conference call. The call came through as scheduled and I began by introducing myself and advising them that the Director of the FBI had established a special task force to take the lead role in these and any future such cases. I have been chosen to lead that task force. So, let me begin by saying, I need all the help possible. I know that most of the work has to be done by those in your departments. So, keep at it in terms of the groundwork that you can do. For now, the only restrictions I think necessary, is that all statements made to the public or news media be cleared through my office in advance. Anyone having problems with that should speak up now, please." I heard no objections and continued, "We are checking the backgrounds of all congressional staff looking for anyone who might fit the profile, and if we identify anyone residing in your areas we will call on you for assistance. We are also monitoring the radio and television media, especially the talk shows, for any loonies that may be out there. Now, I would like for each of you to introduce yourselves and your departments, so that everyone knows who's who." I quickly added, "Let's do it in case order, please, that means Fairfax County goes first."

"Good morning, this is Sergeant Mike Furda of the Fairfax

County, VA. Police Department. I am the one who will most likely be here every morning, in the event I can't be; I will try to get Corporal Chuck Ellis to fill in as he was the first on the scene of Mr. Davis's murder. We don't have anything to add to what you already know, unfortunately."

"A good morning to all of you, from Sergeant Brody Edwards of the Beaufort County, North Carolina Sheriff's Department. Unfortunately, I have to echo Mike's report of nothing new on the murder of Congressman Connor."

"I will say good morning also; this is Sergeant Clarence Smith of the Metropolitan Police Department in the District of Columbia. I, too have nothing to add at this point."

"I want all of you to know that Brody and I are friendly acquaintances from a previous case where a terrorist came here with the intent of cutting off his head. You know that plot was spoiled, because you just heard him talking, what I want you to know is that he has written an excellent book about that experience, which I have just finished reading. It is available on Amazon, and I recommend you get a copy, the title is Beneath the Shadow of the Cross."

Brody laughed and said, "Thanks, Colt, I can use the publicity, the twins need new shoes."

We finished the conference call, and I immediately called the Agent in Charge of the Nashville Region to give directions for security for the funeral of Mack Davis which was scheduled for Wednesday at 2 PM. The AIC turned out to be an old classmate of mine from the academy, named Ron Walker. We caught up on what had happened to each of us since graduation and then got down to business. "I really don't think Islamic terrorists are involved in this case, but we just cannot afford to let our guard down - - the risk is still there. I want you to contact Gene Wilson at the Grassland Heights Baptist Church and arrange for one of your men to be an usher inside the church, where he is free to surveil the crowd. Also, direct the Williamson County

Sheriff to set up detours at Moore's Lane and Concord Avenue to move as much traffic as possible from Franklin Road over to I 65. We need at least three police officers inside the church, and I want enough blue lights flashing outside to discourage any would-be troublemaker. At 1:45 put three men about two blocks north and south of the church, with instructions to slow traffic to a crawl, visually inspect, not search, each car - - just do whatever it takes to prevent a drive-by shooting. The interment will be in Nashville, so make sure there is a smooth trade-off of security responsibilities between Williamson and Davidson County police. I also want a hidden camera as well as a concealed sniper at the cemetery. If someone does take action to harm the family or anyone else at the service, take them out. No hesitation, understood?"

He responded, "We can handle all of that. Don't worry; we will do the job, you have enough to worry about."

That statement proved to be almost a prediction as things heated up in the coming days.

CHAPTER 5

WEDNESDAY MORNING, I arrived at the office just after 7:30 and immediately logged in to our system and pulled up the task force website. The section marked television media was blinking, indicating new activity, I clicked there and saw the headline, Jihadi group claims responsibility for Congressman Davis's murder. Additional lead-in provided by Wendy Rogers, our clerk monitoring television media, read: MSNBC, New York affiliate reported that they had received a videotape, in an envelope postmarked Dearborn, Michigan and they played it on last night's 11 o'clock news. (click here to watch video)

I clicked the space indicated, and a video appeared on my screen. The room seemed to be empty of furniture; a sheet was being held up by someone on either side. There were two shadows cast onto the sheet by spotlights placed to the rear of the individuals. One seemed to be wearing a turban and robe, similar to that of an Islamic cleric, the other taller and larger figure appeared to be wearing typical American style clothing. The first voice, I heard was that of the smaller man and he said, "Allah be praised!" The voice sounded like that of a mid-eastern man who had learned English but had not lost the accent of his native tongue. From that point on, the voices were disguised by some means of mechanical distortion. The older man continued, "Mr. Davis, dared to defy Allah by criticizing the Koran, he paid the price, as all who do not submit to Islam will ultimately pay. We are here among you; we are many, some say over a million, some say as many as 7 million, only Allah knows." The second and much younger sounding voice spoke next, "And we are (a beeping sound) ----ing like rabbits, you are doomed." The first man cleared his voice, as if he did not approve of that remark, and continued, "You will want to identify us, you cannot just call us Your Worst Nightmare."

The tape ended. I replayed it three times, gained nothing of value and kept wondering if they or MSNBC had beeped out the F-word? Hitting the back arrow to get back to the home page, I clicked the mouse to access Helen Burrell info on congressional staff. Her note indicated that I might want to look further into an intern on Massachusetts Congressman Sean McGlocklin's staff. The information she provided was: Jonah Paul Conte, age 25, played linebacker for Boston College, holds the school record for linebackers in the number of repetitions bench pressing 225 pounds. Attended Catholic Theological Seminary for one year before dropping out to join the staff as a legislative intern.

I called Helen to thank her and advised her that I was going to have his phone records looked at as the first step and see where we go from there. "Keep digging there should be others worth looking at," I said. I placed the order to obtain his phone records just in time for the morning conference call. Once we were all connected and I discovered that no one had any information to share, I said, "Well we do have an interesting development. A Jihadi group calling themselves Your Worst Nightmare has claimed to be responsible for Mack Davis's death." I think it is a con job trying to cause shock and fear among all of us. Unfortunately, MSNBC played right into their hands by airing the tape on last night's news. I will send it via e-mail in the next few minutes. Mike, you will need to include it in your evidence file, the rest of you will get it as a courtesy copy." I decided not to

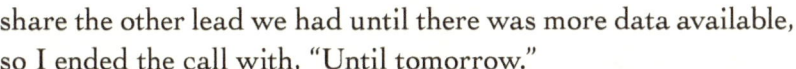

share the other lead we had until there was more data available, so I ended the call with, "Until tomorrow."

Within minutes after hanging up, my phone rang. It was Brody, "Hey guy, I understand you are going to try to get down here this weekend, right?"

"I am going to do my best, but it's not a sure thing."

"Well, how about this as a plan. BJ and I want you both to come to dinner here at 5:30. There's something that might happen in our department in the next few months that just might tickle your interest. Hopefully, we can get a few minutes after dinner to discuss that privately. You can put your stuff in the spare room, get acclimated to the place, I will give you a key to the back door, leave a light on for you and you can stay out as late as you want to. What say you?"

"Sounds like a plan to me. Let's hope I can make it."

"Colt, you do know what today is, don't you?"

"Yes, it's February the 14th," then it hit me, Valentine's day. "Thanks for the reminder, I'm ordering red roses as soon as we hang up."

"You are welcome; I wouldn't want you to be called Prince Chump." He gave me the 800 number for the local florist and hung up.

The florist assured me that the roses would be on Ellen's desk before she went to lunch. I had the card read from Prince Charming. With a big sigh of relief, I went back to work.

I decided to listen to one more of congressman Alvarez's speeches and selected one marked Police Academy Graduation – November 2017.

It was a good speech, lasting about 22 minutes, and I especially liked the way he ended it. He made some excellent points, reminding the graduates that every year someone in law enforcement gets entangled with criminal elements, seeking easy money and bringing shame to themselves, their families and to all of us. "Don't let the criminal element bring you down to their level. If you are in this business to get rich, you are in the wrong business," he said. About midway, he began to focus on the problem of sanctuary cities. He reminded them that some would work for elected officials who think that they should provide sanctuary to those who have broken the law. "Some of them will even claim that their actions are biblically based. Nothing could be farther from the truth. Sanctuary cities in the Bible were never used to protect the guilty; they were for the purpose of protecting those who had accidentally committed a crime. Such people ran to those places, seeking protection of, not from, the law, from those who might take revenge under the eye for an eye system then in existence. They were placed in legal custody until their cases were adjudicated. The concept of providing sanctuary to those who are apparently guilty of breaking the law is absurd." Later he said, "I know that you who are just getting started in your careers will find it difficult to stand against such pressure, so let me address my next remarks primarily to those at the top." He turned and gazed into the eyes of each official on the stage behind him before turning back to the microphone, "It only takes one official with balls to arrest any elected official who orders you not to uphold the law and charge them with malfeasance, to put an end to this insanity."

At the end of the speech, one by one, until about half of the class rose to give him a standing ovation. Only one of those on the stage stood to applaud. I sat there musing, good speech, and it was certainly courageous of him to take such a stance. But, could such a position be the reason for his murder? My gut tells me, no.

At noon, I went across the street to the hole-in-the-wall Asian fusion, primarily carry-out restaurant (misnomer). At the counter, I was greeted by an elderly Chinese looking man, wearing a black skull cap, and sporting a four-inch-long goatee, who said, "I take order, prease." I ordered a cup of hot and sour soup, egg roll, and a small Mongolian Beef stir-fry took the order to one of the three tables provided and sat where I could see the entrance to my building. I had finished the soup and egg roll when my cell phone rang. Seeing that it was Ellen, I said, "Hello beautiful."

"Hello my prince and thank you for the roses, they are gorgeous."

"You are welcome, but I must confess that it had not even occurred to me that today was Valentine's Day until Brody reminded me. I'm sorry to say that I did not send you a card."

"Well that makes us even, I did not send you roses. But you should receive a card in today's mail. Be sure and check the mail when you get home. What are you doing right now?"

"Oh, - - I'm sitting in this really elegant Chinese restaurant. The hostess is wearing this beautiful black silk ankle length dress that has a slit all the way up to you know where. She is bending over me with a very alluring look and asking, "Is there anything I can do for you?"

"Well, tell her to back off, you are spoken for, and I know martial arts."

Then I described the place where I really was and the one who had waited on me, and we had a good laugh.

Back at the office, I had a message to call Helen Burrell. I did, and she related that the phone record of Jonah Conte showed several connections to the Davis landline number and almost daily contact with one of three cell phone numbers listed under the Davis family account. I thanked her and told her, "I am going to place an order to look at his financials and have that info delivered to you. Look for any large deposits and the purchase of airline tickets from here to Nashville. If you get a hit on the latter, check the dates against Mack's travel and speech schedule and then call me."

"Are you thinking, what I think you are thinking? When the tom cat's away, mice play."

"No, that may be true in some cases, but I don't think so in this one. I will admit that she is pretty foxy for a 55-year old, but I do not believe she would have an affair, especially with someone young enough to be her son. We have to check out all possible leads, is all I am really saying."

Back on our web page, I clicked the icon for radio media that was blinking and found the message: "Colt, we need to talk. Vanessa.: So, I dialed Vanessa Norman's number. "Heh boss man," she said. "Look, I am getting so many hits that need checking out, just from Limbaugh, Hannity, and Ingle we can keep a couple of agents busy for days maybe weeks if we look at the other shows, who knows how long it will take."

"Okay, I will ask Olsen to assign the two agents we had previously agreed on and have them contact you."

"I hate to see us wasting the time of our best agents chasing down what I know will be dead-end leads, but I guess it must be done. It will be boring work, but most of these kooks can clear themselves by answering a couple of simple questions as to their whereabouts on certain dates."

The evening mail contained a big red envelop which I opened eagerly. It was a not too mushy Valentine with a sweet handwritten note that read, "I went shopping and bought some pretty things, which I am sure you will approve of if you ever get to see them!"

I dialed her home number to thank her, thinking her present was a whole lot better than mine. Our conversation was very personal and will, therefore, remain very private; I hope you understand.

Thursday morning's conference call was nonproductive, and I told everyone that we would discontinue future calls until and unless something significant breaks. Shortly afterward Helen Burrell called to say, "The financial report on Mr. Conte shows nothing out of the ordinary. His credit card records for the last few months show several charges to United Airlines for trips from Dulles International Airport to Nashville. I checked those dates against Mr. Davis's speech itinerary, and they matched. In other words, Mr. Davis was out of town when Mr. Conte went to Nashville."

My first thought was, "Oh crap; there goes my weekend." I thanked her, hung up the phone and pondered my next moves. This is the best lead we have; it must be checked out even if it ruins my plans. I even considered calling Gene Wilson to see if he could shed any light on the matter, but decided against that. Going for the direct approach, I dialed the number for Congressman Sean McGlocklin's office and asked to speak with Jonah Conte. When he came on the line, I introduced myself and advised him that I would like to ask him some questions relating to the recent deaths of several congressmen. I waited for a second or two, and when he did not answer, I said, "Would you prefer that I come to your office or would you like to come to mine?"

"Actually, I would prefer to handle it over the phone, if possible. I am alone, and I know that personal calls to staff members are not recorded. If you are not comfortable with that, I will arrange to come to wherever you say."

"Alright then, I need to advise you that our phone conversation will be recorded, are you okay with that?"

"Yes sir," he replied.

"Where were you on the morning of February 7th, and can anyone verify your answer?"

"Oh my God, am I a suspect in Mack Davis's murder?"

"Just answer the question, Mr. Conte."

"I slept late that morning, woke up about an hour late, was immediately sick, then I nursed my hangover for at least an hour and finally made it to the office just after 10 o'clock, and, no there is no one who can verify any of that. But, before we go any further, let me say that I am quite sure I can have my presence verified at the time of the other two deaths you are investigating. There is no way I could kill the father of the love of my life. You see, Jimmy Davis and I are lovers. The reason I got so drunk the night before was due to our fighting over him coming out of the closet. I want to make him my wife in a legal marriage ceremony, but he is afraid that would ruin his father's political career. I have my faults, but I am not a killer."

I asked a few more questions and was satisfied that he was nowhere near the scenes of the other two murders. We ended the interview: he is relieved that he was no longer a suspect, and me having mixed emotions. Relieved that we would not have to cause the Davis family any further emotional upheaval and yet disappointed that we were no closer to finding the real killer. After further reflection, my mood brightened with the knowledge that the potential roadblock to my weekend had been removed.

The rest of the week was fairly routine. I spent most of my time in reviewing media input, monitoring the increased political name and blame bickering coming from both major parties and in briefing Jim Olsen with no real information to report. He had called the Speaker of the House of Representatives asking him to warn all Congress that we likely had a serial killer who was specifically targeting them. This was more cover your backside than necessary as I am sure everyone up there was already on high alert.

Certainly, the entire political arena was wound tight. The Louisiana Attorney General was leading a coalition of states in urging federal judges to support the President's Executive Order to punish so-called sanctuary cities. The US Attorney General had appeared on Hannity and urged all law enforcement officials to arrest anyone who orders them not to enforce any federal law. "If you don't like a law, you take the required steps to change or cancel the law; you do not disobey the law," he said. The chatter from an afternoon TV show called the View was almost funny, with four of the left-wing panel members absolutely positive the killer would turn out to be a Republican who is determined

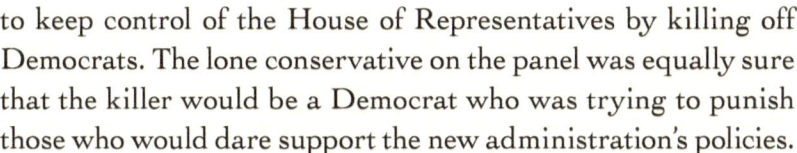

to keep control of the House of Representatives by killing off Democrats. The lone conservative on the panel was equally sure that the killer would be a Democrat who was trying to punish those who would dare support the new administration's policies.

Late Friday I called Jeanette and told her, "I am taking the weekend off, please tell the boss I do not want to be contacted unless there is a major breakthrough on these cases, or another congressman bites the dust. Did you get all that?"

"I do take shorthand, you know. I might clean it up a bit before I give it to him."

"What needs cleaning up?" I asked.

"Well, biting the dust seems a bit crass."

"You are absolutely right; I am just in a hurry to get to Little Washington."

"Oh, it sounds like maybe there is a new love interest in your life."

"Could be and maybe I will tell you about it when I am in a better mood."

"I hope it goes well for you, Colt - - you deserve a good break. I wish you well."

CHAPTER 6

M Y ALARM RANG at 5 AM because I wanted to get an early start. I showered, shaved and dressed in blue jeans, white socks and slip on deck shoes with a long sleeve plaid shirt, all that in about fifteen minutes. On the way to the car, I went through my mental checklist, as is my habit. Cell phone in the front shirt pocket, black suede jacket draped over left arm. Sunday outfit, including dress shoes, right here I thought as I hung them in the back of the car, directly behind my seat. Placing my briefcase on the back seat, I mentally ticked off the things I knew were in it. Change of underwear, pistol, ammo clip, toothbrush, etc., satisfied that I had what I needed, I started the car. The dash clock showed 5:25, I'm satisfied. I only made two stops, one at Fredericksburg where I went through the Hardee's drive through to get a country ham biscuit and coffee and the other when I pulled off I - 95 at Weldon, for gas and a much-needed pit stop. I sent Ellen a voice text from that last stop and another when I stopped at a red light as I entered Washington. I didn't want her to be surprised at my early arrival. Pulling up in front of her house at 11:28, I thought, "I must have broken some speed limits to get here this fast."

She was not surprised, in fact, she had slipped on a windbreaker and met me halfway to the house, with a warm embrace, I might add. I liked the idea that she was not worried about what the neighbors might think. A few minutes later, I was thinking how glad I was that the neighbors couldn't see the steaming kiss we both were enjoying. We leaned back to look at each other, I said, "It is so good to be with you, you look beautiful."

"Did they teach you to lie like that at the academy."

"No lie, just fact, ma'am."

"Come on back to the sunroom, the sun is shining in on the couch, and I want to give you a head massage that is guaranteed to relieve stress." She sat on the couch and instructed me to lie down and put my head in her lap. Then began to slowly run her fingers through my hair, front to back with one hand, while the other started at my sideburn and went slowly up and around my ear then down to my neck. "My daddy loved for me to do this," she said.

"I can see, why. You have magic in those fingers. I could get used to this sort of treatment."

"I hope you do, get used to it, that is."

My next conscious thought was, I have been asleep. "How long? I said."

"About an hour," she replied. "And don't you dare apologize, you needed that, and I enjoyed every minute of it. Now, let's talk about the plans for today. First, I have a breakfast casserole slow cooking in the oven, for lunch, which we can eat whenever you are ready. We are to be at Brody's by 3, the temperature is supposed to be in the 60's, and he has promised to take BJ and the kids out on the boat, the first nice day. We are invited to go along and then he is cooking steaks for dinner. How does that sound to you?"

"Great, I am ready to eat lunch anytime." In the kitchen, the table was already set. She pulled a casserole out of the oven that was large enough to feed six people; it smelled delicious. Placing it of a trivet. She said, "I think you will like this, it has eggs, potatoes, two kinds of cheese, sausage, bacon and country ham sprinkled generously throughout. What would you like to drink?"

I opted for coffee and almost made the mistake of taking a bite before I noticed that she was pausing expecting us to pray. I did a short prayer, noting that she tried to suppress a smile. The casserole was indeed delicious and there was enough left over for several people. We decided to reheat the leftovers for our breakfast tomorrow before church.

We pulled into Brody's backyard just before 3 o'clock to find the boat and trailer hooked to his big SUV, BJ waving, the kids jumping up and down and Brody pointing out where he wanted me to park. As soon as we closed our doors, Hannah ran to give Ellen a big hug, and JJ walked over to provide me with a very manly handshake. Brody said, "Let's get rolling, you can put your things in the house when we get back."

At the boat launch, we all got out, Brody went back to the trailer and started detaching the boat, BJ ran around to drive the SUV, and when Brody got into the boat, she backed the trailer into the water until the boat began to float. Brody gave her a signal, and she gunned the SUV up to the parking area, while he dropped the big 75 horsepower Mercury motor into position, started it and idled over to the pier where he expertly threw a line over the post. It was evident that they had gone through the same process many times, and had the system down pat. We all helped get the life jackets out of the rear of the car and Brody yelled, "Don't forget the bucket." She held up a five-gallon bucket for him to see that she had it. I couldn't help but ask, "What's that for?"

"Emergency use only, there is no bathroom on the boat. You never can tell when it may come in handy."

As we pulled away from the pier, Brody pointed to a bluff that provided a beautiful view of the bay and the Pamlico River and said, "That's the spot written about in the Howling at the Moon chapter." I knew he was talking about his book, Beneath the Shadow of the Cross. A few minutes later he slowed the speed and said, I want to show you something else that was in the book. We pulled into a creek, and he went a few hundred yards where he turned to boat around, pointing over to a pier he said, "That is where I was when Donnie yelled, hit the dirt. Unfortunately, that made it easier for Molecki to hit me in the head and drag me into the water." The boat began slowly going back toward the bay, and Brody pointed to a pier and said, "That's the Friedl's pier where he put me into his rented boat and made a clean getaway before we knew what happened. With that said he pushed the throttle forward and down the river, we went. "You see those stakes sticking up over there, a great fishing spot. You know the Pamlico leads all the way to the Atlantic Ocean. In the springtime, the bass fishing is great all along both sides of the river and in the fall and winter the sea bass run up this way from the Pamlico Sound. That's what you ate last weekend. I'm going to swing over to the other side and head back toward town; there are some beautiful homes as well as some modest weekend retreats all along the way."

It was indeed warm for February, but I was also glad that I had my suede leather coat on. I was amazed at the number of boathouses that were built several feet above water level. I commented, "I grew up on the Shenandoah River, but we didn't have anything like this."

"Yeah, these babies have chains and hooks on pulleys with a motor powerful to lift the boats out of the water. Keeps them clean, you don't have to worry about snakes greeting you when you step in, and makes it more difficult to steal them."

As we came into Washington and passed under the railroad trestle, Brody said, "When I was in high school one of my buddy's dad worked for the railroad, so he knew the train schedules. We would walk all the way out to that turnstile and fish from the platform there. It was kind of scary the first few times, but we got used to it. One of the biggest fish I ever caught was right over there. I was using a bait we called a bullhead, it was painted yellow, made out of lead and must have weighed 5 or 6 ounces. I threw it into a school of sea bass, and it never hit the water but went right into the mouth of a fish. It took me several minutes to land that baby."

Now we were in the downtown area of Washington where lots of sailboats and yachts were docked. He pointed out a restaurant with a sign reading, The Waterfront, "That's the most romantic spot in these parts to bring your sweetie," he said. From there we continued slowly up to the bridge where Route 17 crosses the river and then turned to go back to our starting point. It was a delightful hour and a half journey.

Back at Brody's, Ellen jumped out of the car and yelled, "Dibs on the bathroom," as she ran to the back door. BJ and the kids were laughing as they ran close behind her. Brody yelled, "We have three you know." He then unrolled a garden hose and asked me to retrieve the life vests from the back of the car and to put them on the deck of the boat. "I'll hose it all down at the same time, and they can dry on the boat in the garage." I did as he asked then watched him wash everything down and back the trailer into the garage. While he unhooked the trailer, he suggested I take my things in the house and put them in the guest room. I walked into the kitchen with my things, and BJ said, "Upstairs, the 2nd door on the right. It has a private bathroom." While putting my things away, I thought about the description Brody had given in his book for the preparation of steaks before cooking them. Visualizing all the preparations, he would go through assured me that we were in for a treat.

When I came back downstairs, I peeked into the living room and saw BJ in the recliner with her feet elevated, hands on both sides of her belly, and her eyes were closed. Ellen and Hannah were snuggled together on the couch, and I could not tell if they were awake or not. JJ was sitting on the floor in front of the TV engrossed in a children's program. I quickly turned and headed

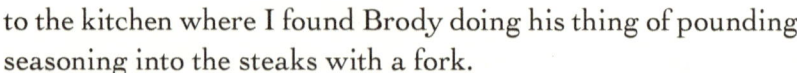

to the kitchen where I found Brody doing his thing of pounding seasoning into the steaks with a fork.

"What's up," he said.

"I think everyone but JJ is taking a little nap, I decided not to bother them, so I guess I'll just have to bother you."

"You won't bother me, besides this may be as good a time as any to have the discussion, I wanted to get to anyway. For the past four years we have requested funding for a special investigator position, and every year it has been one of the last cuts before final budget approval. This year it did not get cut in any of the preliminary reviews. We expect our budget to be approved within the next 60 days and that we will be able to hire someone for next fiscal year which begins in July. The position will have a Lieutenant's ranking, the second highest salary in the department, and I think you would be a shoo-in for the job, should you choose to apply."

"Wow, of all the things I have imagined this conversation might be about, this was not on the list. So, my first reaction is, why aren't you interested in the job?"

"Oh, I was interested and frankly have been working to make myself an attractive candidate for that job for years, but now I have other plans, which I am not at freedom to talk about just yet."

"Um, then I will thank you for thinking about me and just say, I'm pretty sure that would mean a cut in pay for me but, if I don't find this killer soon, I may need the job."

He laughed and then said, "Well if you take into consideration the salary of a certain someone in the department, it might mean a pay raise, if the two were to become one, that is."

It was my turn to laugh, "Not that you are trying to rush me into anything, I'm sure."

"Oh no, nothing like that. You can't break Lashawn and Laverna's record for a short courtship, but you could break mine and BJ's if you get on the stick."

We both laughed so loudly it must have been what awakened the girls because they both came in wanting to know what is going on in here. We looked at each other and gave a small shrug of the shoulders and said nothing. Knowing that will drive them crazy.

BJ said, "Okay, don't tell us – you better not be telling dirty jokes, Brody James Edwards." The twins came running in so I lip synced an I'll tell you later to Ellen. Brody looked up at the kitchen clock, went over to the stove and opened the oven to test the foil wrapped potatoes, and then said to me, "Better put on your coat, the temperature has dropped. We can throw these babies on the grill and finishing those jokes." He threw an impish smile over his shoulder at BJ as we headed out to the patio.

The steaks were cooked to perfection, or at least to my taste, BJ had all the ingredients one could want to put on the potatoes, the conversation though sparse was enjoyable and the company was sweet. Shortly after we finished eating, Brody pointed to the key rack by the back door and said, "Take that key, it fits the back door, we will clean up, put the kids to bed and leave the light on for you." We put up a small resistance, offering to help with the cleanup but they both knew we wanted as much alone time as possible, so we said our thanks and left.

In the car, Ellen said, "Tell me." I related the entire conversation Brody, and I had, and this time neither of us laughed at the line about breaking the courtship record. At her house, we went into the living room, and she asked if I was at all interested in the position Brody had told me. "That is difficult to answer, as I told him it would almost definitely mean a pay cut for me, but the idea of a quieter, less pressure atmosphere does have some appeal. Now, let me ask you a question. How would you react to an offer to leave here and move, say to northern Virginia?"

"I cannot imagine any job offer that would entice me away

from here. Now if you are talking about some other kind of offer, I might give a different answer."

"Okay, let's stop beating around the bush. I am so attracted to you, I think about you when I should be thinking about work and that is so unlike me. And, I will be honest with you, I think a part of the attraction may be this place and these people. I realized this past week that I do not have any friends in my life - - my life has been nothing but work, work, work for the past five years. I am not ready to declare that I am in love or that I want a lifetime commitment, but I am close to that. I promise you that I will be very considerate of your wants and needs should we decide to consider marriage. But I will also say this, should you not be willing to give all of this up and follow me - - that would be a game changer for me. Is that open and honest enough for you?"

"Absolutely open and honest enough for me, and it makes me feel secure in sharing my thoughts with you. I am attracted to you, so much so that it frightens me. You have awakened my flesh, and I am ashamed of some of the thoughts that have flashed through my head all week long. I will admit that I want to drag you up those steps to my bedroom, but my faith and my rational mind tells me that would not be good for either of us. So, we will proceed with caution, but at a good rate of speed, I hope. I will tell you this, the decision to leave my job and this place would be the most difficult one I could ever imagine making, but if we decide to make a life together, I will follow you wherever you think we should go. Fair enough to suit you?"

My response of, "Fair enough" was cut short and smothered by our kiss.

I was back at Brody's by eleven and had an excellent night's sleep. Sunday morning, they were eating breakfast when I came down. I told BJ that I had made the bed and thanked them profusely for their hospitality. BJ said, "You are more than welcome, and I will not wash the sheets until you have used them a few more times. We are expecting you back next weekend."

Ellen and I finished off that fantastic breakfast casserole, cleaned up the kitchen together and went into the living room where she said, "Colt, I know I can trust you with the part of the story that Brody did not share with you last night. It probably will only be a few more days, at the most a couple of weeks, before Donnie announces his early retirement. His wife is having health issues that will demand him spending more time at home with her, and with Brody's reputation, he is a shoo-in to succeed Donnie as sheriff. So, if you take the investigator's job, you might be Brody's boss for a few months but, eventually, he will undoubtedly be the Sheriff of Beaufort County."

"Very interesting, I am glad you cleared that up for me. I certainly would have no problem with working for either of those two men."

We went to church and then to KFC for their buffet lunch and made it back home by 1:30. In the middle of what we had started calling a smooching session, Ellen leaned back and said, "Thursday night is Karaoke night at Smokies. Brody and BJ, Joe and Tilly, and Lashawn and Laverna go almost every Thursday night. Listening to their stories make me so jealous of not being included. You really need to get down here on a Thursday so we can join them."

I laughed so hard; I could tell she was getting riled. "What's so funny about that?"

"Now honey, don't get upset. You have to admit that it came from far out of left field. What would make you think of Karaoke in the middle of a smooching session?"

She chuckled, "I know; you will have to get used to the way my mind works, I do that a lot."

"I will learn to live with it," I said and got back down to business.

A few minutes later she broke off a kiss and said, "Just look

on your left as you leave town, you will see that Smokie's is building additional space, and it's largely due to the large crowds on Karaoke nights'."

With a huge grin on my face, I responded, "Is that so."

As I drove out of town at just after four o'clock, I saw that it was a true statement.

CHAPTER 7

W E LEARNED OF the death of the fourth United States Congressman on Tuesday morning, February the 20th. It was another case of the staff notifying local police that he was overdue at the office. Prince George's County Police entered the residence of Joe Lewis Blevins, just outside Brandywine, Maryland at nine thirty- seven to find his body on the living room floor in a sitting position, leaning against the coffee table. I arrived at 10: 42 to see the body draped with a sheet, and several people dusting for fingerprints all over the room.

The detective introduced himself and began to brief me on what they had so far. He held up a digital camera with a reasonably large screen and said, "Brace yourself." The first picture showed that the deceased's right eye had been plucked out and was hanging from its' socket onto his cheek. The second shot was a view of the rear of his head, which showed that his skull had been caved in by a blow that must have resulted in instant death. Then he said, "This scene had obviously been posed. We know that he was hit in the head over there by the television. You can see the blood right there. He was dressed as if he was ready to go to work. We think he had only been dead about an hour and that his body was posed to indicate that he had been watching porn. I say that because when we accidentally giggled the mouse by his body, the laptop on his legs awakened to a hidden camera shot of a woman masturbating at an office desk. We think both stacks of DVD's, the one over by the TV and the one here on the coffee table are probably porn. The best clue we have is this." He held up the camera to show a picture of the congressman's lower body. "His pants were unzipped, and this note was stuffed in his pants, with about half of it in view." He held up a small plastic bag with the note, and I saw that it read, Matt. 5:29. I knew that If thy eye offends thee, pluck it out, had to be close to the correct quotation.

I said, "Okay guys listen up. You probably know already that the FBI has taken the lead in cases like this one. I want you to know that I have been assigned the head of the FBI Task Force to investigate these and any future cases. I expect you to continue to work this case just as you would if were we not involved. The only difference being that you will brief me on all activity involving this case and you will not make any public or media releases that have not been cleared by my office or me." I looked around to see that they all were nodding that they got my message. Satisfied that they understood, I continued, "The four deaths are definitely connected in that a citation of a Bible verse had been left at each site. But the motive for each murder does not seem to have any connection. The first congressman was passionate about excluding Islam from our country, the second case seems to be about immigration, the third about sanctuary cities and now this one seems to have a sexual connotation. So, if you come across anything that will shed light on the connection of these cases, please enlighten me. Now, I need you to make a written record of each DVD and the serial number of the laptop and bag them. I want to get them to the FBI lab as soon as I can."

With the evidence in hand, I headed to HQ, stopping thru a Mikey D's drive-thru for lunch, which I consumed as I drove to the Hoover building. I arrived in Olsen's office a little before one and asked Jeanette, "Is he back from lunch?"

"Not yet, but I expect him to walk in any minute now."

"Okay, this is evidence taken from the scene of our fourth

congressman's death. Please get the fingerprint experts to go through all of this trying to id any prints other than congressman Blevins. Then get it to the computer techs, I need them to put as many resources as possible to identify people and or places on the DVDs. Warn them that we think they all involve porn."

Jim walked in just in time to hear the last few words, and said, "Why are discussing porn with my very religious secretary?"

"Just warning her not to peek," I said as I followed him to his office. He chuckled, and I looked over my shoulder to see Jeanette blushing and giving me a wave off. In his office I went through all I knew about the Blevins murder, and we discussed how different the most obvious motive for killing each of them was, yet surely connected by the use of Bible verse in every case. After explaining what I had directed be done with the evidence gathered at the Blevins resident, I said, "This may be the best lead we have so far. I am pretty sure we will find that he was using hidden cameras to spy on his female employees and from the one video that I looked at that could easily make someone mad enough to either kill him or hire someone else to do the dirty deed." I noticed that he was nodding his agreement and went on to say, "This could easily involve the sexual harassment slush fund that has so many people upset. I know that Congress has resisted releasing any information about that fund but, we simply must know if Blevins had any sexual harassment claims filed against him. If he did, every complainant becomes a suspect that we have to investigate fully. The Director will have to give his approval of course, so the ball is in your court on that one. We need that subpoena!"

"I agree, and I will take care of that. I know you are getting frustrated, four murders in two weeks' time and we are no closer to solving any of them than we were on day one; but, you are doing a good job, keep up the good work. We will get them."

Back at my office, I followed the usual routine of pulling up Blevins' biography and reading it several times.

"Joe Lewis Blevins born July 13, 1961, to John and Latisha Blevins, both of whom worked for the Defense Department at various locations in the Washington, DC area. After graduating from high school in 1979 he attended Howard University where he served in the student government and was Junior Class President. He became a member of the Phi Beta Kappa Society and graduated in 1983 with a Bachelor of Arts degree in Political Science. Three years later he earned his J.D. from the University of Maryland School of Law.

"He joined the D.C. Law Firm of Roberts, Roberts, and Landrum in 1986 where he worked until he was elected to the state legislature.

"His political career began in 1990 when elected Mayor of Brandywine, Maryland. He served two terms as mayor before he ran for the Maryland State Legislature and won a landslide victory with over 72% of the votes cast.

"A similar landslide victory occurred when he first won a seat in the US House of Representatives in the year 2000. He has been an active supporter of all legislation to benefit federal employees, who make up a large percentage of voters in his district.

"Mr. Blevins has been recognized as one of the most eligible bachelors in the Congress but has escaped capture over the years.

"He currently serves on the Committee on Transportation and Infrastructure and the Judiciary Committee.

4006 Rayburn HOB
Washington DC, 20515
T (202) 225-8386
F (202) 225-9113"

The next day I was informed that the only fingerprints

on the items turned in yesterday were those of Congressman Blevins. The news from computer technical support was more encouraging. Many of the hidden camera shots were definitely taken in the congressman's office. Two of the women appearing on those videos were identified as former clerical support. Both of those women no longer worked on Capitol Hill in any capacity.

I have decided not to reveal the names of either of these individuals in this book. I will assure you that each of these women was fully vetted. One had returned home to Philippi, West Virginia and the field office reported that she was in the local hospital giving birth to her first child at the time of Blevins murder. The other woman took more time, and effort to confirm her lack of involvement in the murder. I contacted her by phone at her residence in South East DC, on Wednesday morning. She agreed for me to interview her at her home just off Suitland Parkway at 2 O'clock that same day.

I arrived at her modest duplex right on time and she invited me in. After the appropriate introductions, she said, "Let's cut right to the chase, I know you are here about the death of Congressman Blevins, and I do want to cooperate with the FBI, so turn on that recorder and let's get started."

I did so, and she began, "I am not a fan of the congressman, and you will soon know why, but, I did not kill him, and I am pretty sure I can prove it very quickly. You see, every Tuesday, Wednesday, and Thursday I meet two girlfriends at the Dunkin Doughnuts shop just down the street for coffee and doughnuts. We seldom miss meeting on those days and I know for sure we were there yesterday morning from 8:30 until about 9:30. Check it out that should clear me of personal suspicion, I think. Now, let me provide you with some details that hopefully will fill in any gaps you have been wondering about and then I will give you a possible lead, who I honestly do not think killed the man, but you will need to check him out. I worked in Congressman Blevins office as a receptionist/typist for about six months last year. I answered most of the telephone calls coming into the office. There was a recording device located in a wire basket, attached to the back of my desk, hidden from view between my desk and the wall. I could activate the recording with a button on my phone. When I announced an incoming call, he would use a codeword if he wanted me to record that conversation. You need to know that although I could record any call, I could not retrieve the recordings as the wire cage was locked and only he had the key. I didn't test the system every morning, but, I did do so often, and one morning when I activated the button to test the system the light kept blinking so I looked behind the desk to see if I could detect what might be the problem. When I did, I saw another wire box with a recorder that had not been there before. The wiring for that recorder led to a hidden camera under my desk. I knew instantly that the bastard was taking up-skirt videos of me, so, I checked the other desk and found that it too was rigged with a hidden camera. I decided not to confront Blevins, but instead did some research on hidden camera technology. I bought a system and installed it in the bookcase and caught Blevins retrieving the recordings. Then I got myself a lawyer, and we threaten to sue and go public. He settled, I got $250,000, plus legal fees and he supposedly gave up all copies he had in his position. So, now this house is paid for, I have a new car, and I don't have to work for a while, at least. Now, here is the part that you will want to check out. A few months back, I had a live-in boyfriend named Daniel James Mays. He's into break dancing and prefers to go by DJ. One night, I had a little too much to drink, and I was worrying over my belief that Blevins had not turned over all the recordings he had. I told DJ about what had happened, thinking he could put some pressure on Blevins and make him produce any recordings he still had. The next morning, in a sober state, I realized the mistake I had made, in that, I had violated my part of the agreement to keep it quiet. So, I pleaded with DJ not to tell anyone or to make contact with

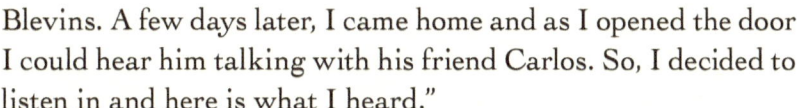

Blevins. A few days later, I came home and as I opened the door I could hear him talking with his friend Carlos. So, I decided to listen in and here is what I heard."

DJ said, "I was at the club last night and who should walk up to the bar but Congressman Joe Lewis Blevins. So, I sauntered up next to him and said, 'My girlfriend used to work for you.'"

"She did, what's her name."

"Her name don't matter, what matters is she thinks you have some videos taken of her, without her knowledge, and that you didn't turn over all the copies you agreed too. What do you have to say about that?"

He looked at me, shrugged his shoulders and said, "Nothing."

"Well, what if I had this switch-blade in my pocket pointed at your balls and threatened to castrate you, would that change your answer?"

He raised his hand above his head and pointed a finger down at me and said, "No."

"The next thing I knew one of the biggest blankety blank N word you have ever seen had me by the belt and the scruff of my neck. He raised me up on my tiptoes and hustled me out of there so fast; I didn't know what was happening. I believed him when he threatened to castrate me if I ever bothered the Congressman again."

Carlos said, "That's too bad, you could have scored some serious points if you had gotten any extra copies from him."

"Serious points, my ass. I could have gotten some serious bucks for those CDs, and she would never have known that I had them."

"They were laughing so hard I know they didn't hear me close the door and go to the bedroom. I grabbed the house key I had given him, threw his wallet and pocket change into his duffel bag along with all his belongings I could find. I went into the kitchen where they were drinking beer, picked up a meat knife off the counter, threw his duffel on the floor and told them to get out and don't come back. I haven't seen either of them since that day. Now, and I may have said this before, I really don't think DJ did it, but you need to check him out."

I thanked her for how succinctly she had laid out everything, knowing she had saved me several hours that I usually would have had to spend to get all that information. I told her that I believe her and was sure that I would be able to clear her from suspicion, as early as tomorrow. I also promised to let her know what we found out about DJ Mays.

Back at the office, I placed an APB on Mays and logged onto the system to go to our web page for the latest info available. Finding nothing of importance there, I checked my return call notes and decided they could wait until tomorrow because the two individuals had probably already left for the day. I decided to go home. I fixed dinner in my apartment for the first time in several weeks, nothing to brag about, just opened a can of chili, got out the sharp cheddar and made a grilled cheese sandwich. Washed it all down with a can of Pepsi. Thinking, I better chew some tums tonight to guard against heartburn, I dialed my sweetie.

Settling back in my recliner, I didn't bother to turn on lights or the television; I just let that soothing southern accent penetrate my being to lose all sense of time. We had a lot to talk about with the new case entering the picture; I was nonetheless amazed when she said, "Colt do you know what time it is?"

"No," I could not believe my watch correctly read 11:30. It did, so we reluctantly said, "Good night."

CHAPTER 8

T HURSDAY MORNING, I awoke at my usual 5:30 time
and began getting ready for work. It was pure luck that I
looked at my phone calendar to realize that today is George
Washington's actual birthday, which was celebrated as a Federal
Holiday last Monday. Since I worked all day that day, today
is going to a holiday for me. It is Thursday. I made two quick
decisions: First, I called in and left a voice message with Jeanette
that I am taking today as a holiday, to put me on annual leave for
Friday the 23rd and that I would not be available until Monday
morning; Second, I am going to take Ellen to Karaoke tonight.
This time, I packed a small suitcase with things needed for the
three, almost four day's stay, threw a Jimmy Dean's sausage,
egg, and cheese croissant into the microwave made myself a
Keurig cup of coffee to go and was on the road by 6:30.

At about 9:30, feeling sort of smug, I realized that I needed
to make some arrangements. So, I hit the voice command button,
and when asked how can I help you? I replied, "Call Brody
Edwards, residence." BJ answered on the third ring.

"Hey, little momma, this is Colt. How are you doing this
fine morning?"

"I'm good, for the shape I'm in, that is. What in the world are
you doing calling me this morning?"

"Well, I thought I had better check to see if my room might
be available for the next three nights?"

"Of course, it is, are you on your way?"

"I am, but I want it to be a surprise for Ellen. I want to take her to Smokies' tonight; I do hope you all are going."

"Well, to tell the truth, we left it up in the air last week. The others are waiting for me to decide because of my condition. But, I will definitely call them all and get it set up for our meeting at 6 o'clock. Oh, it's going to be so nice having the two of you join us."

I thanked her and said, "Goodbye." I opted to stop at Ralph's in Weldon as Brody had often suggested, I do. The North Carolina style barbeque was okay, I think I might still prefer the Kansas City style, but I have to admit, he was spot on about the Brunswick stew and the hush puppies. They were exceptionally good. Once past Williamston, I gave directions to call Ellen Buck's cell and waited for her to answer.

"Hello Prince Charming, what are you doing?"

"I'm sitting here in my office, toiling away. What are you doing?"

"Actually, I'm in the grocery store getting ready to check out with a cart full of stuff. Brody insisted that I take the day off since I got called in on this past holiday to help solve a computer system problem. Why don't I call you back when I'm home and have put all this stuff away?"

"Okay, sounds like a plan. Call my cell, I might not hear the office phone from way back here."

"Okay, it will be about 15 minutes."

"Yeah and maybe you can describe some of those pretty things you bought that I have not yet seen."

"Ha, fat chance of that. Besides, there is not much of them for me to describe anyway."

"Hey, I like the sound of that. Bye, bye, sweetheart."

I slowed down trying to time it to arrive at her house in about twenty minutes. It worked out perfectly as I parked in front of her house and went up to the porch and tiptoed over to the swing where I sat waiting for my phone to ring. I didn't have to wait long. I answered and said, "I felt guilty about not realizing that last Monday was a holiday that I could have spent with you, so I ordered something special for you. Did you check the front porch when you came in?"

"No, I parked around back as usual and came in the kitchen door. Wait, I'll go look right now."

She opened the front door and was looking on the floor, expecting a vase of flowers, I'm sure. When she looked out toward the street she saw me in the swing; she yelled, "Colt McLean, you rascal, I will get you for this." We rushed into each other's arms. It was hard to tell whether she was laughing or crying. The kiss was so tender and sweet; it didn't matter because I knew if she were crying it would be tears of joy.

In the house, I asked her forgiveness for my lying to her. "I just thought it would be so much fun to surprise you and to tell you that we are going to Karaoke tonight." She squealed with delight, and I explained that I had talked to BJ and she was going to make sure that everyone would meet at six. "I assume that the plan meets your approval, then."

"Oh yes, it meets my approval, and you are so forgiven. This has to be one of the best surprises of my life."

We went into the living room and headed straight to the sofa to begin a smooching session. Before long we were lying stretched out, me with my back to the back of the couch, she had the outside in case the phone rang, you know. We were both getting our blood pressure up when she said, "Enough of this, you need some rest." She reached up and pulled the afghan off the back of the sofa, spread it over the both of us and began to give me a head massage. It was evidently, just what the doctor ordered because I was asleep in no time flat. When I awoke and checked my watch, it was just after five which meant we had slept over an hour. I cleared my throat and watched as her eyes began to flutter open, then said, "What in the world are you going to tell everyone?"

"What do you mean, Colt McLean, I'm not going to tell them anything. There is nothing to tell."

"Oh, but there is. You can no longer claim that you have not slept with a man."

She slapped me hard enough across the arm and chest that it hurt. "Ouch, can't you take a joke."

"My virtue is not a joking matter," she said as she jumped up and flung the afghan in my face. I was glad to see that she was laughing when she said, "I'm going up to get ready, you can use the bathroom down the hall."

We all arrived in the parking lot at Smokie's at about the same time, said our hellos and walked in together. It was crowded, and there must have been four people working to get everyone seated. One of them, who I later found out was the manager, waved to Brody and we followed him to a table reserved for eight. Brody introduced us, and then the manager said to BJ, "I'm glad to see that you brought your guitar, that means we are in for a real treat." She grinned without responding, and he said, "We will be featuring music by the decades tonight. So, when you hear the DJ announce the 1950's, I would appreciate it if Joe and Tilly could rush forward to kickoff that section by doing the jitterbug to the tune of Rock Around the Clock. Will you do that?" When they nodded agreement, he said, "Great the crowd will go crazy, I'm sure."

They did too. It was the most fun that I'd experienced in ages. We talked and laughed so much my face was beginning to hurt. BJ awed the crown by playing her guitar, using the plucking method Brody's father had taught her, while she sang Crazy. There were a surprising number of elderly folk there that night, and they indeed enjoyed the expert way Joe and Tilly danced. Lashawn and Laverna duet was also well received. Ellen nor I participated in the singing or dancing, but we had just as much fun as anyone else.

I was surprised that Brody had thought to bring me the

backdoor key so that I could come in as late as I chose too. I asked him if I could use the conference room to get a little work done the next day and if I could take Ellen for an extended lunch period as well. He agreed, we asked for separate checks, paid our tabs and were out of there around 9 PM.

Friday morning, I slept late, for me that is, and came into the kitchen carrying my laptop to find a mommy hovering over her kiddies, encouraging them to eat their cereal. When I reached the table to muss JJ's hair and give Hannah a peck on the cheek, BJ said, "I think today might be the day, tell Brody to stay ready." I agreed to do that and asked if there was anything I could do to help her before I left. She sipped her coffee, waved me toward the door and said, "No but thanks for asking, I will call on you, if I need too."

I pulled into Hardee's, taking my laptop with me, ordered a country ham biscuit and a cup of coffee, asked for the password to their wi-fi and went to a corner table. With my first bite, I thought, "The best biscuit in the world." Logging into the system, I found that DJ Mays had been discovered locked up in the Calvert County, Maryland jail on a drunk and disorderly charge. So, that gives him an alibi, he could not have murdered Mr. Blevins. Next, I checked my notes to get the phone number needed to verify his ex-girlfriend's presence at the time of the murder. After verifying that she was indeed having coffee and doughnuts as she had reported, I called her to advise her that neither she nor Mr. Mays was suspects in the congressman's death.

Leaving Hardee's, I pulled into Ye Olde Sweet Shoppe, once owned by Barbara Jean Edwards, nee Woolard and ordered a picnic lunch to be ready for pickup by noon. On the short drive between Chocowinity and Washington, I called Jeanette and dictated a briefing for Jim Olsen bringing him up to date on the things I had just learned. She said, "Just as I thought, you are

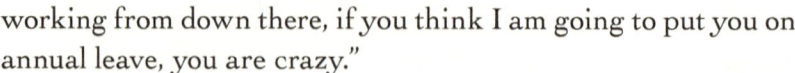

working from down there, if you think I am going to put you on annual leave, you are crazy."

"Okay, thanks, just don't call me unless you absolutely have to."

"How are things going down there," she asked.

"I am so hooked, but don't tell anyone just yet."

"I wish you, the best, and tell her I think she is getting a real catch."

"I'm not sure I am ready to tell her that yet, but I do thank you, and I want you to know that I appreciate all the help and encouragement you have given me these past few years. I will see you Monday."

I walked into the Sheriff's office at about 10 AM; no one was around, so Ellen stood up, leaned across the desk and gave me a short kiss. I stood there with eyes closed savoring the sweetness until I heard a voice echoing from down the hall, "I saw that."

Ellen responded, "Brody Edwards, are you spying on me again?"

"Not exactly spying, just making sure you're being discreet," he said.

I interjected, "Not to worry; she is very proud of her status."

He laughed, and she whispered to me, "Not true, I am actually very tired of it."

I gulped, thought but did not say, "I know what to do about that."

Brody called out to me, "Come on back, now is as good a time as any, to have that conversation we talked about last night."

I closed his office door behind me, sat down in front of his desk and said, "I could use your advice. As I have worked these four murder cases, I have been forced to look at the state of our country, the way the political system is failing us and quite frankly, I see us heading for disaster. There is a danger out there, far greater than a serial killer. I am toying with the idea of writing a book, using these cases to point out some of the danger and to hopefully call attention to something just getting started that if allowed to go unchecked will surely destroy America."

"Wow, and I thought this would be about the job we talked about, that you had decided to ask questions about why I couldn't talk about my not wanting the job, but this is a real surprise."

"Well, you have written a book, a very good one, I might add. I think I can write the story rather quickly; I certainly hope so because time is of the essence. The problem is, I know nothing about the publishing process."

"Okay, I will try to be of help to you. First, you need to know that statistics show the average sales for a first-time writer, in the self-published arena, to be less than 50 copies. You will also need to steel yourself against disappointment and not let your experience affect your friendships. I say that because you will have very few friends who will buy several copies of your work to give to their friends, but you will have more who will never spend the few bucks to purchase it. There are so many people who just do not read books, and there are also many who have no idea that it will cost you more than $5.00 to give them the free copy they expect. Next, I will tell you that self-publishing a book is very easy, Amazon has done a great job in helping me get my book to market. The problem with self-publishing is that you will have extreme difficulty in getting the needed publicity to market your book. I have had several people tell me that my book should be brought to the attention of the Kendrick brothers, Mel Gibson and or Oprah Winfrey, the problem with that is those people are so busy, they have isolated themselves from guys like us. You simply can't get your work before them. So, when I hear you say that you want to attract the attention of America, that tells me that you have to go through a publisher to get the exposure you need. I am considering going that route and have found two companies that I think will do a good job for me if I am willing to pay the price. I will be glad to share those contacts with you. Finally, your habit of journaling will help you greatly; I had more trouble getting started in my journaling habit than I did in writing the book. I hope that helps."

"Yes, it does, and I would appreciate your keeping this confidential for a while, I haven't even discussed this with Ellen, yet."

He agreed, and I went out to tell Ellen that we have a two-hour lunch break, courtesy of Sgt. Edwards. We took off, picked up my preordered lunch, and I drove to the KOA campground and out to that beautiful spot Brody had shown us last week. Walking to the picnic table, I said, "Guess we can't say we will be howling at the moon since it is broad daylight, but this is certainly a beautiful spot."

"Yes, it is, and I am so happy to be spending time here with you. What did you get us to eat?"

Opening the bag, I pulled out the sandwiches and said, "A chicken salad with lettuce and tomato for you, a tuna salad with tomato only for me, chips, and two bottles of Arizona sweet tea. That's it, hope you like chicken salad."

"It will do nicely, thank you. Just being with you is enough to make me happy."

After we ate, I told her of my wanting to write the book, basically the same information, I had given Brody earlier. I did go more into detail about the danger I saw for our country and how my passion for the project was growing day by day. "I guess I will be frustrated more every day because I can't take on such a project until we catch this killer," I said. "The more I think about it; I will need to take a leave of absence until the book is done, yeah that will be the thing to do."

"Maybe you could come down here to write it. My sunroom would be a nice setting for such an undertaking, don't you think?"

"Um, maybe so, we will have to think about that."

I had her back at work on time, grabbed my laptop and went

back to the conference room and pulled up the task force web page. I checked the space assigned to each jurisdiction involved and found nothing of interest. Talked to Wendy Rogers and Vanessa Norman both of whom assured me that our agents are hard at work vetting people they had tagged. Next, I called Helen Burrell and said, "I can't believe we got just the one hit you gave me from the entire congressional staff."

"Strange that you should call at just the moment I am downloading a profile that you may be interested in checking out. I withheld it at first, and you will know why when you read it, but a friend of mine who works on Capitol Hill advised me this morning that and I quote, 'She may be handicapped, but she is as strong as a bear.' Seems to be an unlikely suspect to me, but you should be able to review the file in about five minutes."

I thanked her, hung up and made a pit stop. When I got back from the men's room, the file had finished uploading. It read:

"Sally Matthews

Age 29   Height: 5' 8"   140 pounds

"Registered Republican. She works on Speaker of the House's staff as an Information Specialist. The Speaker described her as brilliant, and incredibly talented at reading body language, mannerisms, facial expressions, etc. He relies heavily on her in polling members of Congress on both sides of the aisle to monitor possible voting positions.

"Daughter of a Baptist Minister, adept at quoting scripture, but usually does so in a scornful or sarcastic manner having turned away from religion after her tragic accident. Graduated from Colorado State University where she was a member of the ski team, specializing in downhill and slalom. Was a leading candidate for the United States Olympic team before her accident. Now paralyzed from the hips down, she has a motorized wheelchair, equipped with a hydraulic device, which she patented, to assist her in and out of the chair.

"Youngest of three children. She is very competitive, especially against her brothers both of whom played college football. She is able to live independently, in her Falls Church apartment. Drives specially equipped van which locks her wheelchair into the drivers' seat position. Able to pull herself up a rope to ring the bell faster than most world-class gymnast (eyewitness account)."

I read through Helen's write up three times and sat there puzzling over what to make of it. A female as the possible killer? I just don't know. She might be strong enough to have pulled it off. The daughter of a preacher - - come on man. Doesn't make sense to me but, she has to be checked out. A good project for Monday afternoon. I went to Brody's office and asked if BJ had called?

"Oh yeah, several times but not the call to say come take me to the hospital. It won't be long she assured me."

"I'm taking Ellen to the Waterfront for dinner, just call if you need us."

At her house, she went straight upstairs to get ready, and I went to the living room, laid down on the couch, pulled the afghan down as cover and was asleep in minutes. I don't know if it took an hour and a half for her to get ready or if she just let me sleep, but it was 6:30 when she nudged me awake with her knee. Sitting upright, I gasped out, "That red dress looks stunning on you - - maybe I should have said you bring out the best in that red dress."

"Either way, I thank you, sir. It makes me feel special when I see you react that way."

"What way?"

"Colt, I know the hunger you are feeling, and that makes me feel wanted, which is a good thing. Although I have to be even

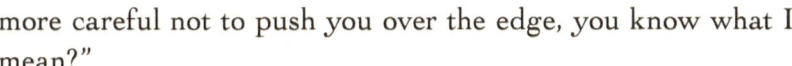

more careful not to push you over the edge, you know what I mean?"

"Yes, I do know but, please feel free to be a little riskier."

Knowing that finding a good parking spot would be unlikely, we decided to walk the four blocks to the Waterfront. Several couples were waiting, but as soon as we walked in the maître d' said, "Right this way sir, your table is ready." Seeing him heading toward what had to be the best seat in the house, I quickly extracted a ten spot from my wallet and discreetly pressed it into his palm as he finished seating Ellen. As I took my seat, Ellen said, "He goes to my church, I called ahead."

The view was outstanding I thought as I looked over a yacht that had to be worth several million dollars docked right in front of our window. The lights were low; she looked so beautiful, I could not help but softly sing, you are so beautiful to me.

Our waiter arrived, introduced himself as Tony and handed us menus. I asked for water for us both and told him we would give our drink order after we decided on the main course. We both ordered the seafood platter called The Captain's Choice with a baked potato and a house salad. Ellen agreed that a glass of white wine would be nice. "We will stick with water as our other drink choice," I told Tony. He brought the salads out immediately, we joined hands, and I said a short prayer while we stared each other in the eyes. A few minutes later, she said, "You see that distinguished looking couple over there, that is Buzz and Chris Latham, you read about them in Brody's book. He has been a good friend to Brody, and I am almost certain Brody will ask him to Chair his campaign for sheriff."

During the meal, I told her all about the Sally Matthews profile Helen had sent me. "What do you think? Any chance that she is a good lead?"

"Who knows?" Then she laughed, "One of many quotes my dad attributed to his father, who died before I was born, was,

'You ain't seen mean until you have met a mean woman.' Why that came to mind, I have no idea."

We finished our meal, paid the tab, left Tony a generous tip, and walked outside with the intent of strolling the several blocks of restored waterfront. We changed that plan quickly, noting that the temperature had dropped several degrees while we ate. Instead, I took her hand, and we walked at a brisk pace back to the house. It was almost midnight when I left for Brody's, and the only thing I have to tell you about the rest of that evening is, "What those pretty things she bought look like remains a mystery."

Saturday morning, I made up my bed and went downstairs to find the Edwards clan at the breakfast table. Everyone was smiling except BJ so, I go over to give her a pat on the shoulder and a quick peck of a kiss on the top of her head and asked, "How are you this morning." She pants out a couple of puffs of breath and mutters, "Having some minor contractions, I think today is the day."

"That is what you said yesterday, you know."

"Yeah, I know, but I'm surer today than I was yesterday."

So, I looked at Brody and said, "I am heading to Ellen's, we may take a stroll downtown, but we will both be available if you need us."

Ellen opened the door for me and said, "Come on in Mr. late sleeper, let me fix you some breakfast."

"That sounds good to me."

"How do you like your eggs?"

"Whatever way you like yours will be fine with me."

"I've already eaten, just tell me your choice."

"Over easy is my favorite," I replied.

"Okay, the bread is in that drawer, pop a couple of slices in the toaster, get the butter and homemade grape jelly out of the fridge, and help yourself to the bacon there. I cooked it earlier and ate a few slices just before you got here. I'll have your eggs fried in a jiffy."

By the time I had the toast buttered and slathered with jelly, she said, "Hand me your plate."

The eggs were as I liked them. As I ate, she stood behind my chair placed her arms around my neck, ran her hands just inside my shirt and scratched my hairy chest. It felt so good, I leaned my head back on her bosom and said, "This feels so right!"

"It does to me too," she responded after kissing me on top of the head. Then she exclaimed, "Oh my gosh, I just realized that I am standing here doing the same things my mother used to do for my father. It is almost scary. She always got up early; brewed coffee had a cup or two while she read her Bible, usually two or three chapters every day. Then she would begin to fix breakfast and eat hers as she prepared my dads'. When he came down, she would stand behind or beside his chair, drink her coffee with him and either massage his shoulders, scratch his chest or his head and occasionally pick up a piece of bacon and place in on his plate. The times I witnessed those scenes, I remember thinking it to be almost sensual. Now, I realize there was no almost to it, and it was most definitely sensual. Often, when he finished eating she would pick up his napkin and wipe his mouth then bend down and kiss him. Then she would place her left hand on his cheek and pull his head over to her bosom. They would stay that way for several minutes; it was as if he was listening to her heartbeat. Now I see why they enjoyed breakfast together so much. Colt, this relationship is getting sweeter by the minute."

"I would like to hear your heartbeat, my dear." She reached over and placed her left hand on my cheek and pulled me to her bosom. "How sweet it was."

We cleaned up the kitchen and then went into the sunroom where she asked me to tell her more about the book I wanted to write. I explained how I wanted to use the serial killings that seemed to be demanding the book be entitled Killing Congress to call attention to an evil force that if left unchecked would require the story title be changed to Killing America. "My biggest concern is that we have become so polarized that people just might be turned off if they think I am saying they are wrong. I have to find a way to get their attention or I honestly believe our democracy will be destroyed."

"Wow, that is some deep stuff. I was thinking the other day about how each side, Democrats, and Republicans, want to win so badly that ethics and morality suffer at the expense of winning."

"So true, actually the fighting to win makes us our own worst enemy. Each side thinks they are all that matters and they forget that they both play in the same league. Hey, maybe I can use a sports analogy like baseball or football to get their attention. Yeah, I will work on that."

Later, I looked out the sunroom window to discover the thermometer was reading above 60 degrees so, I suggested we get some exercise. She liked the idea, and we strolled toward the main street. "There's not a lot to see like most towns businesses have migrated to the malls," she said. At the first dress shop, we stopped to look at the window display, and she said, "This is where I bought those pretty things, I told you about."

"Oh, then I guess if I want to see them I have to go in and ogle a mannequin?"

"Yep, that's right."

I stood there pondering whether I wanted to tease her by going into the store to do my ogling. She moved to the next store. I caught up to find her staring at a beautiful diamond ring displayed in the jewelry store window. We stood there admiring it for several minutes, saying nothing. I don't know what she was thinking, but I almost suggested we go in to look at it closer. My rational mind, told me to hold up, you've only known her two weeks, you know. We moved on, turned to come back down the other side of the street and had made it almost to Market Street when my phone rang. I answered, and Brody said, "Can you and Ellen come quickly, I need you to watch the kiddos while I take BJ to the hospital."

"We are about four blocks from the house, be there as soon as we can." I grabbed her hand, and we jogged the rest of the way. On the way, she said, "Why don't you go ahead in your car and I will pack an overnight bag and join you as soon as I can. You know this could still take a while, and I may need to stay overnight."

I nodded agreement, jumped into my car and pulled into Brody's backyard 10 minutes later. He was helping BJ into the back seat of his police car when I got there. "I'm leaving you the Escalade, with their safety seats, in case you want to bring them to see their sister before bedtime. The keys are on the rack by the back door." I picked up a twin in each arm, and they waved as their parents sped away.

We were in the living room, where Hannah was busily coloring, and JJ and I were on the floor, pushing a dump truck back and forth to each other when Ellen arrived. "I guess they got off okay?"

"Yep, and I have everything under control."

"Don't get too smug old boy; you have no experience in dealing with four-year-old kids. Their moods can change very quickly."

That statement proved prophetical as by late afternoon they were cranky, picking at each other and asking every minute or two, "Why hasn't daddy called us yet?" Finally, Ellen said, "I think I know someone who could use a happy meal and some time at the playground, why don't we go to MacDonald's?" Both kids started jumping up and down yelling, yea, yea. Their moods do change quickly, you know.

We had finished eating, and Ellen and I were enjoying watching them run up the steps and down the slide when Brody called. "I called the house and got no answer; I hope you are not on your way here."

"No, we are at MacDonald's letting them work off some energy. What's going on?"

"It is going to be several hours yet, they had to work hard to turn the baby and have just now allowed her to start pushing. My guess is that it will be between ten and midnight before she makes her debut. If you don't mind putting them to bed, I will get there as soon as I can."

"No problem, Ellen is prepared to spend the night. She will sleep in my bed, and I will take the couch. Don't worry; we will take care of your kids."

He said, "Thanks." And I could hear BJ straining to push as he hung up.

We let the twins play for another half an hour and headed home. Ellen took care of giving them baths and getting them in their PJ's, then announced, "Colt will read to you now."

I proceeded to do from my perch in their daddy's recliner. At bedtime, Ellen prayed a very sweet prayer asking God to bless mommy and the new baby and to let them have a good night's sleep so they would not be cranky when they go to meet their new sister in the morning.

Sunday morning, we had the kids eating cereal when Brody made his entrance. The kids went wild, "Daddy, daddy, did the baby come?"

"Yes, she did. Matilda Ellen arrived at 11:18 last night, she weighs 7 pounds and 3 ounces, is 20 inches long and is so pretty. It looks like she is going to have red hair like her daddy." He sat at the table with a twin on each knee and drank the coffee Ellen put in front of him. As we sat there, Brody told us all about the birth experience, and we planned the rest of the day. He will take the kids to the hospital to see mommy and the new baby. We will wash and dry the sheets, remake the bed and clean the house before joining them there. Tilly and Joe will bring the

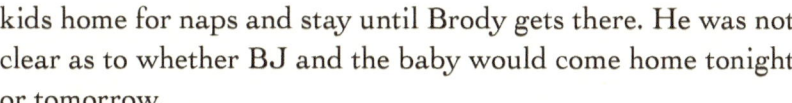

kids home for naps and stay until Brody gets there. He was not clear as to whether BJ and the baby would come home tonight or tomorrow.

After Brody left with the kids, Ellen told me that sleeping on sheets that smelled like Colt McLean had been an erotic experience and that led to a smooching session that we had difficulty breaking away from to get the needed work done. We did eventually get the job done and got to their private room at the hospital by noon. Brody was on the couch with the baby on a unique looking pillow that rested on his knees but seemed to wrap around him; a twin snuggled as close to him as possible on each side. "It's called a Boppy," Ellen informed me. Ellen got to hold her first. When it was my turn, I chucked her under the chin and said, "Thank the good Lord they didn't name you Matilda Jean, I think two BJs, a JJ, and an HJ are enough. We don't need to add an MJ to this menagerie." The adults all laughed and Barbara Jean said, "I agree with you on that."

A quick bite to eat, a much too short smooching session and I headed back to northern Virginia.

CHAPTER 9

WAS HOME BY about 9:30, finished unpacking, did a small load of laundry and completed my journaling just in time to turn on the TV to catch the eleven o'clock news. I was bored after watching about fifteen minutes of local stuff and was reaching for the remote to turn off the TV when a bulletin flashed on the screen: Late Breaking News Follows: Stay tuned. So, I eased back in my recliner waiting for the commercials to end. The evening news announcer came back on with this report. WHSV, TV out of Harrisonburg, Virginia has just reported that Rockingham County Police have investigated the death of the fifth United States Congressman in the last seventeen days. An unnamed informant told the WHSV news anchor Carl Rodgers that he had monitored police broadcasts and had visually verified that they were on the scene at a cabin owned by Alonzo Martinez, Democratic Congressman from Arizona. The congressman's cabin is in a secluded area bordering the George Washington National Forrest. WHSV contacted Rockingham Police who refused to confirm or deny the congressman's death.

To say I was steaming mad would be an understatement, how is it possible that the head of a task force investigating murders of US Congress finds out about the death of the latest victim on late night television. No way should this have happened. I grabbed my laptop, logged on to our webpage - - Oh crap, there it was, and I had just not checked in to our system since early morning. No need beating myself up over it, I'll deal with it tomorrow.

Monday morning, I was still hot under the collar, fortunately, before I made the phone call, I remembered that my anger should be directed at myself rather than the Rockingham County Police. So, I had cooled down considerably by the time they were able to connect me with Sergeant Alvin Dellinger who had been in charge at the murder scene. He put me on the defensive when the first words out of his mouth were, "Agent McLean I was expecting you to call all yesterday afternoon, what happened?"

I was forced to admit that I had been traveling and had not checked our system until after hearing the eleven o'clock news. "So, bring me up to speed, what happened up there?"

"First, let me assure you that the leak to the Harrisonburg television station did not come from anyone in this department. I have already checked that out and found it to be, exactly who I suspected. There is a retired individual living on the next property over; his name is Charley Owens. He monitors all police and rescue calls and loves to be on the scene of any action he can get too. I contacted him this morning, and he confirmed that he had walked over the hill and videoed us working the crime scene and had been the one to contact WHSV. I did not confiscate his video because I don't think he did anything illegal, but if you want me to get it I will?'

"No, that won't be necessary. Go ahead with your report."

"Well, we estimate the time of death to be around noon Sunday, we think that because it started snowing around 1 o'clock and there was no snow under his body. In response to an anonymous phone call, I arrived just before 4 o'clock. I had two spotlights in my trunk that I had not turned in from a previous case, so the video I will send to you is of good quality, I just need your e-mail address."

I gave it to him and asked him to continue.

"You will need to brace yourself as this is a brutal scene. It looks like he went out back to gather some firewood, there were several sticks under his body. Marks on the back of his neck indicate that a Taser was used to bring him down. He fell right beside the chopping block. Either his right arm came to rest on the block, or someone placed his arm there before using the ax to sever his hand and then bury the ax in the back of his head. We found a note clutched in the severed hand that had a bible verse citing Matt. 5:30. I know enough scripture to say that if thy hand offends you cut it off, is close enough to consider that the quotation. We had the cabin dusted for prints, and that report should be available soon, but I don't have much hope for finding anything of use there. The best hope we have of finding additional clues will be to wait for the snow to melt, maybe there will be some tracks under there. At any rate, I have put a padlock on the gate to keep everyone off the property until we can finish looking the place over."

"Okay Sergeant, it sounds like you have a handle on things up there. Just make sure we get a team up there to give the place a good going over as soon as the snow is gone. In the meanwhile, I want you to make a very short statement for the Harrisonburg television station, to confirm the death of Congressman Martinez by an unknown assailant. Do not give any details about how he was killed, nor should you mention the note. At the most, you can use the term brutally murdered. You should confirm that the next of kin has been notified, assuming that you have done so."

"Yes, we have done that, and I will prepare a written statement, and send you a copy for your approval before I e-mail it to the station."

I voiced my appreciation for his work, gave him the information he needed to be a part of any conference calling that might occur in the future, and we said our goodbyes.

About ten minutes later my phone chimed to advise of an incoming message. Sergeant Dellinger had been correct about both the quality of the video and the brutality of the scene. You could see clearly that the hand had landed about three feet from the chopping block, as verified by blood stains over there but the video showed it on the chopping block. The thought of someone picking up that hand and forcing it into a fist to

hold the note, and then burying the ax in his head was so overwhelming

that I had to swallow several times to keep the bile from erupting from my mouth. I thought, "This had to have been done by a seriously angry dude."

I was going over my notes from the weekend and was thinking about how to proceed with the vetting of Sally Matthews when my phone rang. It was Jeanette who said, "Colt, the boss said for me to tell you," 'Get your (you know what) up here now, the Director wants to see us.'

"I'm on my way," was all I said and hung up.

Jim Olsen and I entered the director's office on the 7th floor at exactly 1:30. He rose to greet us and said, "What the hell is going on out there, this is the fifth United States Congressman to be murdered in three weeks' time. Tell me you are about to nail this guy."

"Sir, I wish I could, but the truth is we are not even close. Thanks for your quick work in getting the subpoena for that slush fund info, I have been able to clear all the suspects having to with the sexual abuse angle of the Blevins case. Now, I need you to do the same for the Martinez case, because that also looks like it has the same implications. We are hoping that when the snow melts up at his cabin, we might glean some clues that are now snow-covered. I am just beginning to vet an individual, who works for the Speaker of the House, but that is more a shot in the dark lead than a solid clue. I don't invent clues, sir. We are doing the best we can, and unless you have assets sufficient to provide 24/7 security to every Democrat in Congress, I don't know what else we can do."

"You know full well I cannot do that, but, you need to know

the President is upset about this. He takes his role of keeping the American people safe very seriously, and he has ordered me to keep him fully informed of our progress. You Agent McLean will have a draft report on my desk every day by noon, understood?"

Olsen and I both assured him that we got his message and hustled out of there as fast as we could. Whew!

Back at Jim's office, I reminded him of the criteria we had set for looking at staff members and the fact that we had already cleared Jonah Conte as a possible suspect in the Mack Davis murder. Then I explained that Sally Matthews had met the same criteria and I was going to her office next to begin that vetting process. He nodded that he understood, dropped his head and shook it in a now familiar way, which I took to mean, "What the hell." He waved me out the door.

I asked Jeanette to call the Speaker's office and clear the way for me to enter the Capital Building. Then I opted to leave my car in the garage and catch a taxi for the short ride up the hill to the Capitol Building. I instructed the driver to drop me off at the Independence Avenue entrance to the parking lot. Then made my way into the building via the entrance under the east side steps. I had no trouble gaining admission after a close examination of my credentials. The guard desk then instructed a policeman standing nearby to show me the way to the Speaker's suite of offices. I believe that was more to keep an eye on me because I was armed than it was to be courteous.

At the receptionist's desk, I asked if Sally Matthews was available to speak with me privately for what would probably take less than fifteen minutes. She replied, "Privacy around here is the difficult part of that request, the conference room is in use, but maybe Sandra, her office mate will be ready to take a break. Let me check." She made the call, and in just a few minutes a woman who I assume was Sandra came walking toward me. She said, "Sally says you are welcome to go on back, I will take a break and or wait out here until you are finished."

I walked down the same hall and entered the open door where I found Sally in her motorized wheelchair. I showed my credentials, and told her my name but did not mention the task force. She held out her hand and gave me a very firm handshake and then said, "Don't tell me that one of my stupid brothers has done something to cause the FBI to be investigating them."

"No ma'am, this has nothing to do with your brothers. Could you just tell me where you were on the mornings of February 7th, February 12th, and February the 20th?"

"My God! Am I under investigation for the murder of those congressmen?" Her arms gave a sweeping motion down toward her legs and the wheelchair, and she said, "You can see, can't you?"

"Are you saying that your handicap would have prevented you from doing such things?"

"Hell no! I can do anything most anyone else can do, except walk that is. I guess I was stunned that you would think I could. Most people, especially you of the hairy legs variety, would automatically eliminate me from suspicion. Maybe I should be flattered that you bother to ask the question." She chuckled, and then went on to say, "I was at work here in the office on each of the dates you mentioned. We use a computerized log in system, similar to the old time-clock, that interfaces with payroll to keep our records. You can verify that easily, and Sandra will be able to confirm my presence as we usually keep about the same schedule."

I thanked her for her time and left her with another firm handshake. At the receptionist's desk, I was asked to wait just a minute; the speaker wants to talk to you. She picked up the phone and announced that I was ready to leave now. Evidentially the speaker cleared me to come in because she hung up and pointed toward a door behind her. As soon as I saw his face, I knew he was not pleased with my presence. He left no doubt that was true when he said, "And why may I ask is the head of the

FBI Task Force charged with investigating the death of United States Congressman interviewing members of my staff without the courtesy of informing me first?"

"I do apologize but let me offer you reasons why I did it this way. First, I know you are a busy man. Also, I thought this matter was so trivial and that it could be cleared up so easily, that you would not even know about it, much less be upset about it." I went on to explain that based on the assumption that the killer must be known to all of the victims, we had decided to look at all staff members, using the criteria of strength and knowledge of scripture. "Sally met those criteria, but I think she has cleared herself by being at work at the time of at least three of the murders. I will have to verify that of course."

"Okay, I understand, and I want to thank you for being so thorough. We certainly can't take the chance of letting any possible suspect slip through the crack. There is no doubt that she meets the criteria. I just cannot see a possible motive for her to be the one you are looking for."

"Neither do I sir, but I will say that she demonstrated a bit of a temper. I do thank you for your time and again offer my apology."

He said, "Yes, we have all seen that temper at work at one time or another, but again, what motive could she possibly have?"

We exchanged business cards, and he promised to contact me if he found anything that might be remotely connected to the murders. Outside, I did not see any waiting cabs, and wound up walking back to the Hoover building where I ordered the verification of payroll records of the Speaker's staff. Now there I sat in the middle of rush hour traffic, knowing the trip across 14th Street Bridge to Crystal City was going to take close to an hour; I called Ellen.

With our first few words, I could feel some of the tension leave my body, I told her about that and my day. She said, "Oh I wish I could give your head my magic finger massage."

"I could certainly use that now," I said as I described the way traffic was moving one car length at a time, six rows deep.

"But just think, you got to meet with the Director of the FBI and the President of the United States is interested in what you do every day, wow, I am impressed."

"Yeah, and I get to eat out of a take-out box and ponder what to do before either of those two decide to fire me. Doesn't seem impressive to me."

CHAPTER 10

T UESDAY MORNING, FEBRUARY 27th: My day begins as usual, by logging into our system. Nothing there from any of the police departments involved, the only thing I saw was a request for me to call Mark Fletcher, one of the agents assigned to the task force. I waited until 8:30 just to make sure he was on duty and then called. He confirmed that payroll data supported Sally Matthews claim to be at work on the days in question.

"I suspected that would be the case, but we had to check it out," I said.

"Well not so fast, the fact that she and Sandra Wilson checked in and out within one minute of each other every day, seemed odd to me, so I looked past the several pay periods. After the first pay period in February of this year, their schedules seemed more normal, in that their check-in times were farther apart as I would expect them to be. That norm held for all of January of this year, but from early September until after Christmas of last year I found that they checked in and out within one minute of each other. I mean, for four months two people check in within one minute of each other, every day, and out the same way, I don't think so. It looks to me like they are padding the payroll to get an hour's overtime every day."

"Um, I see your point, and I appreciate your extra effort. If I see anything else about Sally Matthews, having to do with these cases, I will talk to Sandra Wilson to see if we can press

her to break the alibi. We can't afford to spend time looking into payroll fraud right now."

Next, I prepared my daily report for Jim Olsen, including Fletcher's concerns about possible payroll fraud and advised him that I was not taking action on that at this time. As soon as I transmitted the report, I called Jeanette and asked her to tell the boss that he could edit, reformat or do whatever he liked to make that information meet the Director's requirement to keep him informed. "I am too busy, to prepare separate reports for every echelon of the command."

"Okay, - - it's your tail feathers in the crack, not mine."

"I appreciate your concern, just do it."

Then I phoned each of the police departments to bring them up to speed on the latest murder and developments. I tried to encourage each one by saying, we will get a break soon. Hopefully, before another death occurs.

At this point it was necessary to do the tedious repetitive like things that bother all law enforcement agents, I went to the internet to pull up Congressman Martinez biography. There was nothing unusual there so I will not bore you with the details. Going into our records, I found an incident when he was serving in the Arizona State Legislature where a woman had filed a sexual harassment lawsuit against him for inappropriate touching. Even though that suit was later dismissed; I decided to ask Olsen again to subpoena records of any such lawsuits against Martinez while serving as a United States Congressman.

Wednesday morning, February 28th started out as a duplicate of the day before until about 11:45 when my laptop pinged indicating activity on the system. As soon as I moved the mouse to awaken it, the screen flashed a message: Assault on Texas Republican Congressman Casey Champion may have been attempted murder. Incident caught on camera and will air on WJLA at noon. I grabbed the phone, called Jeanette telling her to alert the boss and headed for the conference room.

I turned on the overhead television projection system, tuned in to channel 9 and went to the door to call out, "You may want to watch the noon news, it looks like we have an attempted murder of another congressman. I took a seat at the end of the table and waited for the report to come on. By the time the noon news came on, the room was full of agents and clerical staff.

The report began: "Texas Republican Congressman Casey Champion was assaulted at a luncheon at the Mayflower Hotel in downtown Washington, D.C. this morning. The congressman was hit in the back of the head with what appeared to be a regulation nightstick like those used by most police forces. He is currently recuperating from a concussion in a local hospital where his condition is described as guarded. Mr. Champion was on his way to the speaker's platform to address a group of concerned citizens who are championing the cause of term limits for Congress or as they like to call themselves the TLC. The entire episode was caught on camera, and although it lasts less than a minute, I should warn you that you may want to protect young children from viewing it. To let you make those arrangements, I will say that we have no knowledge of Mr. Champion's views as to term limits, we do know that he has captured nationwide attention in recent days because of his urging the committee on which he serves, The Congressional Oversight Committee, to investigate the FBI for trying to influence last year's Presidential Election. Now we will play the tape of today's luncheon event."

I watched as the Congressman rose from his seat, pulled several sheets from his inside coat pocket, which I assumed was the speech he intended to deliver, and headed to the front of the room. Suddenly, a young man rushed at him and jumped to hit him a glancing blow to the back of the head. They both fell to the floor, but the assailant made a quick recovery, stood and turned for a full facial shot that looked to have been purposefully stopped. He raised both hands in a triumphant manner and yelled: "John 3:16." He immediately ran from the room with the alert cameraman following maybe 20 to 30 feet behind him. We got a good view of him running toward the front door where the elegantly dressed doorman saw him coming and opened the door for him. The doorman evidently realized that something was wrong and then decided to trip the man as he ran by. It was almost comical as the man fell down the few steps to ground level, coming to rest at the feet of a policeman who picked him up cuffed him. The last few frames of the video showed the young man grinning at the camera, which was now right in his face, and saying, "Did I kill him? I did all the others, you know."

The news anchor came back in view and said, "We do not have the identity of the assailant at this time, but we promise a complete report on this evening's news. As I switched the TV off, I heard someone say, "So, our serial killer is a kid who can't be more than 21 years old."

I said, "No, that kid you just saw is not our serial killer. He is either high on drugs or is mentally impaired. Didn't you see the vacant look of those eyes? Besides, he is not big or strong enough to have staged the scene of the Davis murder. No, he is definitely not our serial killer."

I went back to my office and placed a call to Linda Farnsworth, Chief of the Metropolitan Police Department. She provided the following information: Assailant is Benjamin (Benny) Anderson, age: 21, height 5 feet 6 inches, weight 135 pounds, home of record in Norfolk, Virginia. After providing this statistical data, she said, "There is no way this guy could have committed the murders he is claiming. He isn't strong enough and frankly, I am pretty sure he is totally deranged, and it looks like he just wants attention."

"My assessment, exactly," I replied. "See if you can find his medical history, I don't think I need to get involved in this one."

About an hour later, Linda called me to say, "We were able to contact his doctor, a psychiatrist named Ira Blankenship.

He provided proof that Benny was under evaluation at Saint Elizabeth's Hospital for the past sixty days and was only released last Saturday. So, he could not have committed the first four murders. The doctor also stated that Benny was released on a trial basis, over his personal objection, and stated his intention to see that Benny is confined for a very long time."

"I certainly hope so. Thanks for letting me know. Oh, by the way, what is the latest on Mr. Champion's condition?"

"I was told that he would be released from the hospital tomorrow morning."

"Thanks again, and keep up the good work. At least you won't have us underfoot on this one."

"Hey, it's been nice working with you. You are welcome in my bailiwick anytime."

Thursday morning, March 1st: I was pleasantly surprised to find the subpoenaed information on Congressman Martinez was available so quickly. The slush fund had paid out over a million dollars to four women in the past year for claims made against Congressman Martinez. The data provided included the names of the four women, the amounts paid to each, but did not provide details as to why the payments had been made. I called Helen Burrell and tasked her with getting current addresses for the four individuals and asked her to call me when she had the information. Then prepared my daily report for Jim Olsen and when Helen called back, I told her to advise Mark Fletcher and Clyde Harding, the other agent assigned to the task force, that I would be there to meet with them within thirty minutes.

After delivering my report, I made my way downstairs to meet with my guys. I emphasized that this information could be the break we needed to get this serial killer, but we have to make sure the four women and any person(s) close to them are fully vetted. Looking at the current addresses, we found that three of them had moved out of the area. Clyde spoke up immediately saying, "For family reasons I need to be here this weekend, if you two don't mind I will do the one living in Arlington." Both of us sort of shrugged our shoulders indicating that we had no objections, then Mark said, "Well I would like to cover the one in Lynchburg, that will give me a chance to visit Liberty University for the first time since I graduated." I looked at the two addresses left, one of which was in Plymouth, North Carolina and said, "I guess I get stuck with this one." I felt like Brer Rabbit getting thrown into the briar patch, Plymouth is only 30 some miles from Washington and my damsel. The last address was in Sumpter, South Carolina which I found out via a Google map search was just about two hundred and seventy miles and would take approximately 4 hours and 30 minutes to navigate. I made plans to loop down that way Sunday evening and do the interview on Monday morning.

That night when I called Ellen to tell her that I had work in Plymouth Friday afternoon and that I might even carry over a day or two, she was ecstatic. "That is so good; I was afraid you would not be able to come with that bungled attempt on the Texas guy."

"No, that is a non-issue for us, the poor guy is a mental case and totally removed from reality and our cases."

"Please try to get here as early as possible Saturday afternoon; Brody has been saying all week that I had to give you some time off to go fishing. I want you to have that opportunity."

"That sounds nice, I plan on spending all nights there even if I have to return to Plymouth the next day."

"Well, in that case, I want you to sleep here in my guest room. Brody has been complaining about the baby's keeping him awake at night."

"Um, maybe I'll get to see those pretty things after all."

"Hey buster, if you keep talking like that you will be hearing a baby crying all night."

"I promise, I will behave."

"I knew you would of I wouldn't have made the offer."

We agreed that it best not to make plans, other than the fishing outing until I knew how much follow-up work would be required. We signed off with our now customary kissing sounds.

Friday, March 2nd: I pulled up to the designated address in Plymouth to a lovely rambler situated on what I estimated to be three acres. Very nice, I thought. This baby would go for about a million dollars in Northern Virginia. I rang the doorbell and was greeted by a much older woman than I expected. When I mentioned the name of the person, I want to talk to she replied, "Oh no, that's my daughter, she turned and yelled toward the back of the house, "You've got company." She left me standing on the porch awaiting her daughter's arrival.

I showed her my cred pack, and she said, "I've been expecting a visit from you guys."

"Is there somewhere we can talk privately," I asked.

"Yeah, come on back to the kitchen, Mama is watching her soap reruns, she won't bother us."

My first question was, "Where were you on Sunday afternoon from between 1 and 3 o'clock?

"I was right here, alone I might add. But I did take Mama to church that day, and there are several hundred people who can attest to that. She went to lunch with her crowd, and I came home. I'm sure you know that I could not have driven to Virginia in time to murder him, but, I will admit to thinking about doing so many times before I won my settlement."

"Next, I would like to know the names of everyone you have ever told about the incident."

"That's pretty easy because there are only four people who know the whole story. My lawyer and the three other women who collaborated with me in filing our complaints against him. I'm sure you probably have their names already. Look, I was in a very precarious position at the time the incident occurred. It happened just a few months before my divorce was final and I didn't want my cheating ex-husband to benefit in any way, so I waited several months to file my claim. My own mother doesn't know the complete story. To guard against my ex-husband finding out about it I told her I got a small insurance settlement relating to an automobile accident."

"Where there any eyewitnesses to the incident?"

"The answer to that is both yes and no. I mean it happened in a crowded restaurant at lunchtime. How many realized what was going on, I can't say, several obviously knew something was wrong. But only one of my fellow complainants knows the full story. Here is what happened. During lunch, we were seated in this round shaped booth; he ran his hand up my skirt. I squeezed my legs together fast enough that he didn't reach home plate, but he got close, and he whispered in my ear, 'You must be getting pretty horny by now.' I contemplated screaming or slapping him, but instead slipped my steak knife off the table and pressed it to the back of his hand. He didn't move, so I kept pushing harder. He finally withdrew his hand, and I saw him using his napkin to stop the blood flow. Back at the office, my friend wanted to know what happened and I told her. She related her story of how he had groped her, and it was her idea that I should bag up the skirt which had the knife hole and his blood stains. That turned out to be a deciding factor in our winning the awards we got."

"So, you are sure that only the three women you mentioned before, plus your lawyer know the whole story. I am particularly interested in any male, brother, family member, or even a lover who might want to seek revenge."

"I am positive those are the only ones. No lovers, I'm going to keep drawing alimony as long as possible. My biggest regret in this whole matter is that we thought we were hitting him in his own pocketbook, but now I know the settlement was made with taxpayers' money. Which is despicable!"

I wrapped up the interview and was in Washington by 4:30. Having talked to Ellen on the short drive, I was not surprised to smell dinner cooking as soon as I walked in the front door.

After a sweet reunion, I couldn't resist opening the oven to see what smelled so good. I reached for a pot holder and raised the pot lid to see a pot roast, with plenty of potatoes, onions, and carrots simmering in gravy. "Whoopi, my favorite," I shouted. It turned out to taste as good as it smelt. I actually enjoyed helping her clean the kitchen, I rinsed the dishes, handed them to her to load the dishwasher and double checked to make sure the stove was off before we headed to the couch in the living room.

Later I got my first look at the upstairs, where I discovered three bedrooms and two baths. I dropped all my stuff on the bed in the room she said was mine and followed her to the master bedroom. It was huge, had a queen size bed, a big walk-in closet and a sitting area with a recliner and a medium sized TV. The master bath was large also and had apparently been upgraded to include a jacuzzi tub as well as a separate shower. When we came out of the bathroom, I walked over to her bed, pulled down the covers and bent down to smell the sheets.

"What are you doing," she yelled.

"Just checking to see if my smelling your sheets affected me like you said you were affected by sleeping on sheets that smelled like me."

She slapped me on the shoulder hard enough to cause me to yell and then pushed me out the door. "Good Night, and go to your room and stay there, you, big lummox."

"Good night you sweet thing."

Saturday's fishing trip was a huge success; I caught only one fish, the largest bass I had ever landed. Brody estimated that it weighed over 7 pounds. After he told me that one that size was better baked than fried, and knowing he had planned a fish fry, I decided to release it. But, let me back up and tell you the whole story. I was using a single hook bait called a silver spoon casting it into shallow water close to the shore when the big boy hit it. On the third jump out of the water, he stood on his tail and shook his head so vigorously that he was able to free himself. I had a tight line, and the bait came right toward me and hit the side of the boat at my feet. Brody laughed and said, "He threw that one right at you, big boy."

"That's not the least bit funny," I retorted.

"Yes, it was definitely funny. Now, if you want to catch him again, here's what you do. Take that spinner off and use that Jitterbug bait there. Wait a minute and keep watching that same spot. I bet he returns, and if he hits that thing, he will not be able to spit it out."

I did as he suggested and sure enough about a minute later I saw a tail fin sweep back and forth as if to make a bed for the big guy to lie in ambush. My cast was accurate, hitting about 18 inches from where I thought he was. As soon as I set the reel and the bug turned, he hit it. That was the most fun ever; he cleared the water three different times trying his best to shake off that hook. It took about five minutes to get him in the boat, and yes, I have a picture to prove I caught him. I am ashamed to say that I have another picture showing Brody and his eight bass, each weighing over two pounds. But the thing that really made the day a success was the way Brody, and I bonded. I was able to tell him all the things I was thinking about, my hopes for the future and he helped me see things more clearly, and I believe even understand myself better. How neat it is to have a best friend like Brody Edwards.

Later, I went back to Ellen's to clean up and then we joined Joe and Tilly back at the Edwards at 5:30. Ellen had cooked a big pot of baby lima beans; Tilly contributed a large bowl of fried okra and BJ had two pans of cornbread. All that added to the fish fillets I had watched Brody magically create with an electric knife made a feast that I hope is making your mouth water. Oh, I forgot to mention that Brody had added special seasoning, I know he put some cayenne pepper in the batter, to give it just the right amount of bite. What a great meal and the fellowship was exceptional also.

Back at Ellen's, we wound up in the living room recliner, with her sitting in my lap, feet dangling over the arm of the chair and her head resting on my right shoulder and chest. It was so sweet. I shared how much I had enjoyed being with Brody and related his suggestion for further investigation the cases and how I was going to give that priority on Monday morning. Later as we reached the upstairs landing, I said, "I've been wondering, is there a waiting period in North Carolina between getting a wedding license and the actual wedding?"

"And you accused me of coming out of left field. Where in the world did that one come from?"

"I just want to know. Why don't you call the courthouse Monday and check that out?"

"I already know the answer. There is no waiting period required."

"That's good. See you in the morning," I said as I closed my bedroom door.

She yelled from behind her closed door, "I bet no one ever called you Mr. Romantic."

I yelled back, "No but I'm still a work in progress. Good night Princess."

If she answered, I couldn't hear her.

CHAPTER 11

SUNDAY AFTERNOON I reluctantly kissed Ellen goodbye after explaining to her that I had to go to Sumter, South Carolina to do one more interview, and that I needed to get back to Virginia as soon as possible.

The trip to Sumter was uneventful and thankfully the Holiday Inn had held my room as I arrived later than I had expected. The next morning, after a surprisingly good nights' sleep, I called the lady I needed to interview and she gave me directions to her house, stating that she was glad that I was here. That surprised me.

I rang the doorbell at precisely 9:15 Am. She answered immediately, and I was amazed to see a surprisingly small but beautiful young woman who couldn't have been more than 28 or 29 years old. I presented my ID, and she invited me inside.

I began with the fact that I was there to ask her questions relating to the death of Congressman Martinez. She replied, "I have been expecting someone to come ever since I heard of his murder."

I went on to explain that although I know that you were involved in a sexual harassment case against him, I am not aware of the circumstances concerning your claim against him. I have however interviewed one of the other complainants in the case, and she shared her story with me. I would like to hear

what you are willing to share with me about the events that led to your winning your case against him.

"Okay, I don't mind so much if you will assure me that there will be no public disclosure that would have my name involved?"

I gave her my assurance, and she began her story.

"I had only been working there for two weeks when he asked me to stay late one evening to help research files to obtain data for a speech he was to make in a few days. Everyone else left the office by 5:30 that day and he asked me to bring him a copy of a speech he had given to the Rotary Club in Phoenix last April. When I found it and brought it to him, he was fixing a shaker of Martini's and offered me one. I had become a frequent drinker in college and readily accepted his offer. After drinking the first one, I remember him asking me to get something else for him, but that is all I can remember until several hours later. I must have passed out because the next thing I remembered was being on his couch feeling woozy, hungover and confused. He was at his desk, and he said, 'I see you are awake, I'm sorry that I made your drink a little strong. You did a very nice job before you went to sleep. I will give you a ride home in a few minutes, so just relax and try to sleep off the buzz.'

About thirty minutes later he drove me home to my apartment in Arlington, Virginia. Going up the walk, I remember sort of stumbling, and he reached down and caught me before I fell. He grabbed my breast and lifted me up, and I remember thinking, how tender my breast felt. He quickly removed his hand, and so I said nothing about it. At the door, he asked if I was alright, and offered to come in if I needed him. I thanked him for the ride but refused his offer of further assistance.

Inside, I knew that I needed to sober up, so I turned on the Keurig and fixed a cup of black coffee. That helped me to think more clearly, and so I went to get ready for bed. When I took off my dress, I noticed that my panties were now reversed so that the label was on the outside. I knew then that I had been

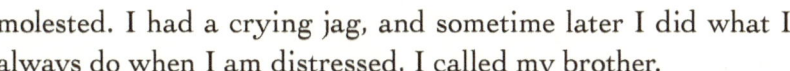

molested. I had a crying jag, and sometime later I did what I always do when I am distressed, I called my brother.

Now, I need to deviate from my story to tell you about my brother because I am really worried that he might be implicated in the Martinez murder. Here are some things you need to know about Jimmy. My dad is known as Big Jim Dalton, of Dalton Construction Company. Jimmy has always been referred to as Little Jimmy Dalton. Let me assure you that there is nothing little about Jimmy. He makes Big Jim look small in comparison, but people still call him Little Jimmy Dalton. He is two years older than I, and he has always been my protector. Jimmy had a very high fever when he was about three years old, and we have always blamed that fever for causing his less than stellar mental condition. He can't do things like complicated math, but he is extremely capable when dealing with machinery and carpentry. He is in every sense a gentle giant. He dresses like a hunter, almost always wearing Cammie's and construction boots, but he can't stand to kill an animal. He loves to fish and will keep ones needed for a family fish fry, but he will not clean the fish. So, I will tell you that he might be able to shoot Mr. Martinez or even do a 'lop-ectomy on his lower brain' as he has threatened to do, but he would be devastated if he had to deal with a dead body. Do you understand what I am trying to convey?"

"I'm not sure that I do, but please go on."

"Okay, back to the story. When I called Jimmy, he instinctively knew what I should do. He directed me to call a cab and have it take me to the emergency room at Arlington Hospital, where I was to demand a checkup to determine if date rape had occurred. He instructed me to withhold all information from inquiring officials until we could get legal advice. I did as he suggested.

The blood tests indicated that Rohypnol, one of the most common date drugs, was present in my system. There was also sperm in my vagina. There was no doubt that I had been sexually assaulted while unconscious.

The next morning, when I did not show up for work, a friend called to check on me. When I told her that I wasn't feeling well, she began to ask pointed questions. To make a long story short, she suspected what had happened and told me about some others she knew who were in the process of taking action against Martinez. I joined them in the suit and we all got a large settlement. I never went back to work there and came home within weeks.

Jimmy was okay with the idea that we had hit him in the pocketbook, but later when he found out that the settlement had been at taxpayers' expense, he made the threat I mentioned earlier. Now, here is what bothers me. Jimmy has been missing for almost a week; no one knows where he is, and he isn't answering my phone calls. I am afraid that he may have killed Martinez and if he did, he is probably holed up in some motel, drinking himself into a stupor so that he doesn't have to face reality."

She was now crying so that she couldn't talk. I told her, "If you have accurately described your brother, he could not have murdered Mr. Martinez because it was a very horrific act of violence." I then asked a few more questions, got her e-mail address and promised to keep her advised on our efforts to find and question her brother.

In the car, I pulled up directions to I-95 and headed home. Called in an APB on Jimmy Dalton as a person of interest in the death of Mr. Martinez and settled into an expected 8-hour drive.

Tuesday, March 6th: At the office, I went through my usual routine with the same disappointing results as previous mornings. Wrote my report of the Plymouth and Sumter interviews and uploaded it to the system. Then called Jeanette as soon as I thought Olsen would be there, only to find that he had gone to coffee with one of his counterparts. So, I asked her to tell him that I need three agents for about three days and if he can have them available to meet with me by 10:30 it would be a big help. Next, I called Fletcher and Harding to get some idea of what they had encountered with the other two complainants. Both indicated that their reports had been uploaded, evidently since I last checked.

Mark Fletcher's report: I arrived at the subjects' address in Lynchburg, Virginia at 10:36 Friday, March 2, 2018. Her husband answered the door and responded to my request to speak to her, "I'm sorry, my wife is unable to speak, she is under hospice care, and is not expected to live much longer."

I showed him my cred pack, and he said, "Well come on in, I assume you are here about the Martinez murder."

"Yes sir, we have to check out all possible leads, and since your wife was involved in a sexual harassment claim against him, well, I do have a few questions, if you don't mind." Following is a summary of our conversation: "The sexual harassment incident occurred around 7 PM August 28, 2017. Martinez had asked her to stay late to type a speech he was to give the following day. She finished typing the speech and delivered it to him in his office at 7. When she placed it on his desk, he came around behind her and pinned her to the desk and grabbed both her breast and squeezed them very hard. She screamed, and he told her that was useless as no one could hear her. She knew that he intended to rape her and when he moved his right hand down to grab her between the legs she was able to get her hands down to the desk and push back enough to slam her spiked heel on his toes. He let her go, and she was able to push him to the floor and get out of there. A week later a friend told her about her and another ladies harassment claims against him. They worked together to get their cases heard. Unfortunately, for us, she got the breast cancer report just weeks later. She had a double mastectomy in late September and found out about a month later that cancer had spread to her ovaries and other organs. She thinks that his touching her was the root of all her problems and she wanted to strangle him, her words, not mine. He also admitted that he had thought of doing him in after she passes, but I am so glad that someone else beat me to it. He stated that he had not left the house for more than an hour in the last week and that absolutely no one else, other than the attorney and the three other complainants even knew about the incident. I verified with hospice workers that he was telling the truth. No further action deemed necessary."

Harding's report was not as sad but more succinct. "The sexual harassment incident occurred on July 13, 2017, at approximately 1:15 PM. The congressman asked her to bring him a file from the cabinet behind her desk. When she placed it on his desk, he complimented her on how much he liked her business suit. She stepped back away from the desk to give him a better view and did a little courtesy as she thanked him for the compliment. He quickly got up from his chair and grabbed her right in the crotch, with enough force to raise her to her toes. She screamed, he let her go, and she kneed him between the legs as hard as she could. A co-worker rushed into the room to find him on the floor, writhing in pain and holding his privates. The complainant stated that she preferred a woman's touch to that of a man's. I checked out her alibi and that of the co-worker who was present at the incident. They both have ironclad alibis. Nothing here boss."

I delivered my daily report to Jeanette, who advised that "The three agents I had requested, should be down there by now."

They were there when I arrived, and we got right down to business. I explained to the five of them that I was going on the assumption that there is someone who knows something about those five men that we do not and that they must have obtained that information within the past few months. "I want you to each choose one of the cases, go to the office and explain what we are looking for. I want a list of names of everyone who met or talked to those men, for longer than a few minutes, over the last four months. You may exclude short calls of congratulations and thank you, those sorts of things, as well as family contacts. You need to make sure that every staff member who knows about such meeting or phone conversations is present to give their input. I think our killer will show up on all five of those lists. I will have them scanned into a spreadsheet and sorted alphabetically, to see if we can id all who made every list. Got it? Any questions?"

There were none, so I ended the meeting by saying, "I need those lists quickly, gentlemen."

Next, I checked on the APB on Jimmy Dalton. Records from his credit card charges showed a gas purchase at Foster's Exxon in Verona, Virginia and at a Super 8 Motel in Roanoke, Virginia both on the 24th of February. So, we have him in the area of the murder, that is some progress.

I had just pulled out my phone to call Sgt. Dellinger when it rang and showed that he was calling me. I answered with, "Hey I had my phone in hand getting ready to call you when you called, what's up?"

"The snow has melted up here at the cabin, and I have found some interesting but confusing prints. I think you or someone from your office should come see what you think went on."

"Tell me what you have, and I will decide who to send."

"Well, there are these huge boot prints that lead from behind a tree to the left of the back door over to the wood pile where the body was. I suspect that the prints are from at least a size 15 shoe, and maybe even bigger. I could tell that the man had knelt by the body, quite possibly to remove the taser from his neck, but then they led away from the house in what looks like a running pattern. I saw that he had slid into a hiding position behind this large oak tree some fifteen yards away from the body. There is a pile of puke behind the tree, which I have bagged for DNA

analysis. By the way, there was almost another pile of puke made in that process."

"I hear you, been there, done that. Okay, here is what I think happened. The prints are probably those of Jimmy Dalton, a brother of one of the women Martinez victimized. His sister has described him as a gentle giant who intended to cut off Martinez's lower brain. I suspect that he was there to do that dirty deed when the real killer arrived, which means he probably was an eyewitness to the murder. So, I don't think it necessary that we come up there. Here is what I want you to do. Check every motel from there down to where I-64 intersects I-81 and find Jimmy Dalton for me. His sister thinks he will be inebriated, trying to forget the horror he experienced."

"Okay, we will get right on it. It makes sense to me because we know the phone call notifying us of the murder came from a cell tower. We were able to identify that it came from a phone with a South Carolina area code, but interference prevented the identity of the entire phone number. I'll get back to you as soon as I can."

By late afternoon I had received a call from all five agents telling me that each office was resisting putting that much time and effort into the task. They all claimed that they had to serve the people in their areas and some had to bring newly appointed persons up to speed. I responded, "Get as tough as you need to, I need that information. I will compromise, by dropping off September, start with the first of October and insist on at least four hours of the Chief of Staffs' time each day until it gets done. Let's see how far we get by Thursday."

CHAPTER 12

⟶◈⟵

WEDNESDAY, MARCH 7ᵀᴴ: Started out as a pretty ho-hum day. I talked to and arranged for the agents to turn in their collected information each day and for the technicians to start scanning them into an excel spreadsheet. That might save a little time, I thought.

Then I received a call from Helen Burrell that revved things up several notches above ho-hum, when she said, "We may have something worthy of your attention. Congressman Walter Farmer, a Democrat from the Detroit, Michigan area, has just made a rather stunning announcement on the house floor that he is switching from the Democratic Party to the Republican Party. Give me about fifteen minutes, and I will have a bio and that speech uploaded to the system for you to view."

The biographical information included a picture of a very handsome black man with salt and pepper hair of medium length, a nice, not too bushy mustache, and a great smile. His personal data showed him to be 58 years of age, a graduate of Michigan State University, having served 25 years in the United States Air Force. First elected to Congress two years after retiring from the Air Force as a Lieutenant Colonel, now serving his third term. Married at age 45 to a fellow USAF officer and they have a 12-year-old son.

I clicked to watch his speech; he began: "I am the son and grandson of Democrats, before that, I don't know of my family political choices because they were not allowed to vote. In my short lifetime, I have witnessed some discrimination and have been hurt by injustice shown to others. All of these things have made me the man I am today. I am not here to complain; I am here today to tell you some of the things that brought me to the point that I am announcing my decision to change my party affiliation from the Democratic to the Republican Party.

"For years I have wrestled with the thought that the Democratic Party panders to my race by giving them handouts, usually referred to as benefits, or charity, which actually reduces their incentive to work and pull themselves out of poverty. If any of you doubt this charge of pandering, I invite your attention to the way the Democratic Party supports illegal aliens. The only plausible explanation to support illegal aliens over and above our own citizens is to eventually obtain their vote.

"I know that many of you are effectively tuning me out and that you will refuse to listen to what I have to say now that you know where I stand. I will none-the-less plea with you to listen carefully. Look around you, at the large metropolitan areas where crime is out of control, poverty and unemployment are at all-time highs, and the local governments are facing bankruptcy, and you will find that they are all run by the Democratic Party and have been for a very long time. This should tell you that the policies of the Democratic Party are not working. Things just get worse and worse the longer they are in control. Because the big and bigger government espoused by that party consume resources that could and should be going to help the people in need. We need good sound business leadership in all of our communities.

"I have had my Christian principles trampled upon by a party that supports Planned Parenthood, making the abortion of millions of babies more easily obtained in the name of women's rights. And a party that even supports late-term abortion, including the killing of a baby partially exiting its' mothers body. I know the black church is alive and well, I see the way my brothers and sisters in Atlanta handled that shooting in their church by a young white man. My heart goes out to them for the way they showed their faith in the almighty. But, I also call out to the black church, it is time for a mass Christian exodus from the Democratic Party.

"To the black community, I call out, check your allegiance. Do your homework. The two most important pieces of legislation affecting us as black people have been the 13th and 15th Amendments to the Constitution giving us freedom from slavery and the right to vote. If you bother to check you will find that the Democratic Party did not support either of those while the Republican Party gave them both overwhelming support.

"I would now like to address the black caucus and indeed all Democrats by saying your behavior at the last State of the Union Address by our President was the straw that broke the camels' back, or if you will, led me to decide to change parties. You sat there with you fancy scarves on, looking all pious and righteous without the courage to applaud the outstanding achievements announced by our President. The fact that you could not bring yourselves to cheer for the fact that black unemployment reached an all-time low reflects on your personal character as well as on the party you represent.

"Now, I want to address both political parties. We have lost our way. We have become enemies, and that simply must change, or we will lose our democracy. I will remind you that we are not supposed to be two different teams with separate goals. We are on the same team, all Americans. We should be viewing ourselves more like the offense and the defense rather than separate teams. We all need a refresher course in Civics. The Biblical admonition that a house divided against itself cannot stand is absolutely true. We have to find a way to cooperate rather than to tear each other down.

"I would also like to appeal to all of you to stand up for the rule of law. We have to defeat this attitude that local politicians can offer a haven to lawbreakers. A lawless society always impacts the weakest in the community. We cannot allow gangs and thugs to be in control. In my 25 years in the Air Force, I witnessed several cases where the careers of young enlisted men were adversely impacted by things as minor as leaving a confidential, the lowest classification of material, out of the safe at night. They were punished rather severely, by a loss of rank, pay and a history that detracted from there records for years to come. Some were imprisoned even though the documents were found by security checkers and the documents were not compromised. Now we have a situation where a former Presidential candidate has mishandled materials classified as high as Top Secret, and the material was likely compromised, and that person has to date escaped any punishment. I call on all of you to uphold the law and ensure that all who violate the law get equal treatment under the law.

"In coming days, I will be presenting legislation that will prohibit the giving of economic assistance to any other country when such assistance must come from borrowed funds. This country has for years given billions of dollars to help countries around the world. All of those funds were borrowed and thus became a burden on the US taxpayer to repay the funds. Consistently going deeper and deeper into debt to help those who will not or cannot help themselves is insane. You would not do that for your own children, why would we continue to do it for those who do not even like us. Please note that I have no intention of placing a ban on the giving of military assistance to other countries. I am making that distinction because we must keep updating our military capabilities and it makes good sense to utilize excess equipment and manpower to help our friends.

"Finally, I appeal to all of you to join me in supporting our duly elected President in his effort to apply sound business practices to help make America Great Again. He is sacrificing his own wealth for the good of our country; he deserves our support. He does not deserve our hatred or our resistance."

When he finished speaking, I sat there thinking, "Is this a good time for him to make such an announcement. I wonder if it crossed his mind that we have a serial killer on the loose, who has murder five Democratic Congressmen as of this date? Does this man need our protection?"

I decided that he just might need our protection, at any rate, we cannot afford not to provide such protection. This gives us our first chance at being proactive. If the killer does come after him, maybe we can trap him and hopefully prevent another murder. I set about making arrangements to interview Congressman Farmer.

We met Thursday morning in his office in the Rayburn Building, and he was shocked when I suggested he might need our protection. "Honestly, it never crossed my mind that someone, especially a serial killer, might want to kill me for my decision."

"Well sir, all we know is that the killer seems to be targeting Democratic Congressmen, for what reasons, we have no clue or idea. It just seems logical to think that your announcement might cause him to look at you as a possible next victim."

"Whoa, that is upsetting, to say the least. Yet, I have to agree with you. Do you want me to hunker down and stay out of sight for a few days, or what?"

"No, I want you to keep your current schedule and plans. Don't change anything, just be more alert than you have ever been. I have with me the biographical sketches of the five agents that will be assigned to assist you. Look them over thoroughly so you will recognize them on sight. They may or may not be close by, but I assure you one of them will be within sight of you at all times."

I obtained his personal cell phone number, his home address

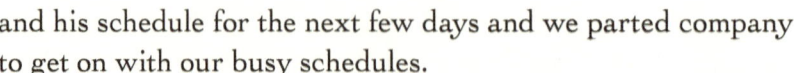

and his schedule for the next few days and we parted company to get on with our busy schedules.

Back at the Hoover building, the techies reported that the first day's collection had been entered into the spreadsheet and that it looked like they would have everything ready for me early Friday morning. When I delivered my daily report to Olsen, he informed me that the Director had given him a message for me.

"Really."

"Yes, he received a call from the President, who asked him to 'tell McLean not to get discouraged, I believe he will get this guy soon.'"

"Holy mackerel, the President of the United States knows I am in charge of this task force and takes time to encourage me! That blows my mind!"

"I was very impressed, I've never known that to happen in my thirty years of service."

I got out of there as soon as I could and placed a call to Ellen as I drove back to my office. When I told her what had happened, she squealed, "Oh, that is so special. I guess your head will swell and I will find it harder to get you to leave the FBI now that you are known to the President."

"I don't know about that, but you might have a bigger area to work your magic finger routine on."

"I'll be glad to give you that treatment no matter the size of your head. Oh, by the way, Brody said to tell you, 'Spring comes early in Chocowinity.' He went fishing this morning and caught a large string of bass and took them to the "hood" as he refers to the black neighborhood, where most of his church members live. He always goes to Miss Sally's first; she was Aunt Hannah's best friend, you know."

"No, I didn't know that, but I can see him doing things like that. He has such a good heart. Anything happening about the potential change or about the budget passage?"

"Nope, not that I know of. Brody and Donnie have been

silent on the first issue, but both have expressed confidence that the budget will pass to give us funds for the new detective position."

"Okay, I'm getting ready to enter the parking garage and will probably lose connection with you anyway. So, kiss, kiss."

The weather forecast at noon warned of a storm approaching from the south that is expected to bring sleet and snow, possibly as much as 3 to 4 inches. "So much, for spring coming early," I thought. The day was slow and boring with the exception that Helen Burrell called to say that she would have the spreadsheet loaded, sorted and ready for my inspection by the time I arrive in the office tomorrow morning. Slow and boring didn't last long enough. At 3:23 Clyde Harding called, "I'm pretty sure someone just took a shot at Walter Farmer. We are hunkered down behind the speakers' podium at the Lincoln Memorial, and I have called for backup."

"Okay, I'm on my way. Stay on the line with me and talk when you can but take charge there and get him escorted where ever he wants to go, office or home. I'll keep listening."

I could hear Clyde directing Metropolitan Police to get transportation for the Congressman as close as you can, now! Then he said to me, "He was walking toward the podium to speak but tripped over the wiring and stumbled forward. He said, 'I heard something whiz right over my head' and I saw the microphone explode. I'm pretty sure it was a bullet that hit it."

I remembered his schedule showing that he was to give a short speech on Thursday afternoon, but I couldn't recall the purpose, so I asked, "What was the occasion?"

"It was in commemoration of the 53rd anniversary of the Civil Rights March on Montgomery, Alabama in 1965."

By the time I arrived on the scene, the crowd was dispersed, Metropolitan Police and FBI Agents were swarming around locating pieces of the microphone and searching for a spent bullet. After almost an hour of looking for the bullet with no success, we assembled the pieces of the microphone which showed clear evidence that a bullet had done the damage. Tracking the direction, the bullet would have come from only revealed that it could have come from a passing vehicle or from the nearby Potomac River. We were unable to confirm either possibility.

I dialed Mr. Farmer's cell number, and we talked for several minutes. He felt sure that it was a bullet that whizzed over his head, "To close for comfort," was the way he described it. He opined that "It has to be a professional hit job paid for by a big donor to the Democratic Party or - - Oh, God, I don't even want to think about the other possibilities."

By dark we still had not recovered the bullet, so we called off the effort, to be resumed the next morning.

I left the office just in time to catch the dry cleaners before closing, to swap my dirty shirts and a suit for cleaned ones, and on to the Golden China for take-out. At home, I turned on the TV to catch the evening news and broke out the chopsticks. Looking at them, I thought how my proficiency had improved over the years, I mean, I am no Mr. Miyagi, I can't catch flies with these things, but I can sure eat General Tso's chicken quite well, I'll have you know. It was just after 9 o'clock when I called my sweetie.

"I hate to tell you this, but I will not be coming this weekend. With the weather like it is and the things that are close to popping here, I just don't think it would be wise for me to leave the area."

"As much as I hate for you not to come, I agree. I don't want you on the road in these conditions. It started sleeting here about 4 o'clock, turned to snow around 5:30, and it is still coming down. We have the main intersections sanded and or salted, but it is dangerous out there. Donnie has ordered double shifts for tonight and tomorrow. It is amazing how much havoc a couple of inches of snow can do around here. Especially when there is a sheet of ice underneath it."

"You be careful, I assume you will walk to work tomorrow."

"Definitely, I almost always do. That 2 and a half blocks each way is the only exercise I get except on the three days I force myself to go jogging."

We talked on for over an hour before I called it a night in order to do my journaling and prepare for tomorrow.

Friday, March 9th: The spreadsheet was finished and revealed only two names that had visited all 5 of the now deceased congressmen. The first name was that of Harold Richards, identified as a member of the Democratic National Committee; the other was that of Sally Matthews, a staff member of the Speaker of the House of Representatives. Neither of the two names surprised me; I was sort of anticipating that Sally would be on the list. It took me a while to determine how to proceed, so I called Jeanette and told her I was working on a new lead that I would include in my next report, but that she should tell the boss to give a nothing has changed report to the Director.

Next, I called the number provided for Harold Richards, when he answered I identified myself as head of the task force investigating the deaths of 5 members of Congress. He said, "I have heard about you, and I'm glad to know that you are working on them, do you have any good leads?"

"Well, let's see. I'm calling you because I see that you met with all five of the deceased in late November. Can you tell me what those meetings were about?"

"Seriously! Are you saying I am a suspect?"

"No Sir, that is not what I am saying. We believe the killer knows something about those men that we do not know, and that thing might be the reason for their deaths. You met with all of them, so I have to ask you a few questions, which I believe you can answer sufficiently to direct our attention elsewhere."

"I'm sure I can and besides I know I can account for my whereabouts at the time of most of their deaths."

"Good, then my next question is what was your purpose in meeting with them?"

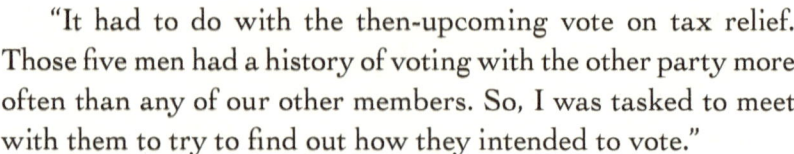

"It had to do with the then-upcoming vote on tax relief. Those five men had a history of voting with the other party more often than any of our other members. So, I was tasked to meet with them to try to find out how they intended to vote."

"Did you get the answers you wanted?"

"No, I mean I got answers from all of them, but they were not necessarily the answers I wanted."

"Then some of them voted in favor of tax relief?"

"None of them would commit one way or the other, so I assumed that some would vote for it. Look, Agent McLean, politics is a dirty business, but as far as I know, no one has killed a member of Congress because of the way he or she voted. If I was upset enough to do that I would have killed them before the vote in December."

"Of course, that makes more sense than to wait and do it after the fact. Now let's just get you to state your whereabouts on the following dates, and I will check that out and not have to bother you any further."

He answered my questions, I thanked him and hung up. Looking out the window, I saw the vender's truck parked in its usual spot and decided to run down and get lunch. As I stood in line to order my Italian Sausage with peppers and onions, it started sleeting. I grabbed my sandwich and a Pepsi and headed back upstairs in a hurry.

When I finished eating, I dug the Speaker's business card from my wallet and dialed the number he had given me. He answered right away, saying, "Agent McLean, what can I do for you?"

"Well sir, I hope you will be willing to help when you hear what this is about. I have reason to believe that we need to look more closely into Sally Matthews. We think that she may have lied about her whereabouts on certain dates and I want to interview her office mate Sandra Wilson to see if I can break her alibi. I would like to do that this afternoon in her office without Sally's presence or knowledge. Can you arrange that?"

"I think so, let me work out a plan, I will need some help from the staff, and I'll call back in a few minutes."

"Thank you, sir, I appreciate that."

While I waited for him to call back, I called Mark Fletcher and arranged for him to meet me and drive me up to the Capital and then drive my car back to the garage and to pick me up again when I was finished. It worked out perfectly, from a timing standpoint, as soon as I hung up from the Fletcher call the speaker called me back.

The Speaker said, "Okay, here is the plan: at 2 o'clock Jeanine will take Sally downstairs to participate in a planning session for a surprise party the girls are cooking up. That should keep her out of here for about 30 minutes. We will make sure Sandra is available. You should wait at the guard desk for a message to advise you that it is clear for you to come up. How's that for a short plan?"

"Sounds good to me, I will be at the guard desk before 2 o'clock."

"Okay, I will have you cleared for entrance."

"Thank you, sir."

It went like clockwork, just as planned. I walked unannounced into Sandra Wilson's workspace at five after two. She was startled and became very nervous almost immediately. "What are you doing here again, Agent McLean?"

"I am here on a very serious matter, Sandra I assume you are aware that lying to an FBI agent is a federal crime, are you not?"

"Yes, yes, I think so, of course, I do know that."

"Good, then let me tell you that I have reason to believe that you lied to me previously when you confirmed Sally's presence here at the office on certain dates."

She began to tremble all over; her hands were shaking so badly she kept dropping her tissue and she started crying.

Finally, she choked out, "Maybe I had better get an attorney before I say anything else."

"I think you should consider that very carefully. Let's say you might have lied the first time, but that you want to correct it now and there is no lawyer involved then I could and would agree to overlook the previous statement. Also, since I am busy investigating murders, I do not have the time or inclination to pursue payroll fraud. Now, if a lawyer is present, he certainly would look out for your best interest, but I would then be forced to take further action on both the lying and the payroll issue. It seems to me that you would be best served by telling me the truth without a lawyer present. What do you think?"

"Oh, I want to do what is right, but can I trust you?"

"I am a man of my word, I promise you that if you do what is right and tell me the truth, I will do what I just told you I would do."

She perked up and said, "Okay here is what happened. Last year when my husband lost his job and was out of work for over three months, we were about to lose our car, when Sally came up with the idea to get me paid more hours. She was working on a special project that had overtime authorization, and she chooses to come in early every day. She used my password and logged me in early every morning. Those extra dollars kept us from losing our car, and we made it through that mess. So, when she asked me to return the favor on three or four days last month, I was happy to do it. On the days in question, she came in several hours later than the records show." She then collapsed into her own lap and began sobbing loudly.

I assured her that she had done the right thing and told her that I thought she should arrange to leave the office before Sally returned.

"Oh God, yes, I can't face her now," she said.

"Let me go talk to the Speaker a minute. I'll ask him to

release you due to weather conditions and walk you out. I hope you are not driving today."

"No, I take the bus."

I talked to the Speaker, telling him that she had recanted her story about when Sally arrived at the office on specific dates. She is very upset and should not be here when Sally returns. He agreed and then I asked about Sally's parking situation. He told me that she has a handicapped parking space very close to the building. I related that I wanted to surprise her and would wait for her near her van if he would agree to release her early.

"Done," he said.

I went back and found Sandra with her coat and purse, ready to leave. We made it out, and I walked her to the bus stop and waited for her to board. "You did the right thing," I said as she got on the bus.

As I stood under that light pole waiting for Sally, I was really glad that my overcoat had a stocking cap and clip-on ear muffs in the pockets. The snow now completely covered the parking lot and I was shivering by the time I saw her wheelchair approaching the van. When I saw her reach into a bag snapped to the handle of the chair and pull out her car keys, I stepped forward and said, "Sally, I have evidence that you were not at the office at the times you stated on the dates of several of the murders. What do you have to say about that?"

"I don't have to say anything about it. But, I will say this, unless you can place me at the murder scenes, and you can't, quit trying to pump smoke up my ass." She had activated the remote to cause her chairlift to put her into the van when she began that statement. My phone rang, and I reached into my pocket to answer it as she pulled away.

It was the Speaker. "I was thinking after you left and so I pulled the report Sally gave me last November in response to my request for her to poll all Democrat Congressmen to see if we could depend on any to vote with us on the tax relief bill.

There were only five who agreed to meet with her, and they were Davis, Connor, Alvarez, Blevins, and Martinez. They are all dead now. Is it possible that she is the killer for whom you are looking?

"Yes sir, it is quite possible that she is. I am already aware that she met with each of those men and I am also aware that she lied about where she was at the time of several of their death's. She just left here with a smirk on her face after telling me that I could not place her at the scene of any of the murders. Well, as I stand here talking to you, I look down at a print that absolutely proves she was at the scene of two of the murders. Look, sir, you are not to tell anyone what I have just said to you. I need you to e-mail a copy of that report and to await further instructions. You might want to watch the eleven o'clock news."

I called Mark Fletcher. "Come get me as quick as you can; I am freezing out here." Then I placed a call to Chuck Ellis of the Fairfax County Police, he answered and confirmed that he was on duty. "Good, I know who the killer is, and I want you to be the arresting officer."

I gave him Sally's address in Falls Church and advised him that he would need a special conveyance to transport her in her wheelchair to the Fairfax County Jail. "Be careful, do not turn your back on her, she can stand, and I'm sure she has a blackjack in that satchel snapped to the right arm of her wheelchair. Arrest her for the Davis murder only and be sure to video record your reading her rights. Get the crime lab guys out there to make a casting of the bottom of her chairlift on the van. I'm sure it is an absolute match for that found on the scene of the Davis murder. Get the van into a compound and ensure that it can't be tampered with. Tell the lab guys to take care with the purse like thing; it probably has DNA evidence in it from some of the other victims. Make sure no one talks to her until I get there, which will probably be another hour or more."

"Way to go McLean, and thanks for letting me in on the

arrest. I should be able to get there by the time she does. See you at the jail."

Then I called Olsen, "We have identified the killer, and Fairfax County Police are in the process of making the arrest. It is Sally Matthews, a member of the Speaker of the House's staff. We are only charging her with the first murder that of Mack Davis, but I am sure that will lead to eventually charging her with them all."

"Are you sure about this? What evidence do you have?"

"Yes, I am positive we have the right person. First, she lied to me about her alibi of being at work at the times of three of the murders. I broke that alibi by getting her office worker to admit that she signed her in as being at work but she really got there about three hours later. Next, you remember that weird print at the Davis farm, that none of us could identify, it is a perfect match for the bottom of the chairlift of her van. The only weak link in our case is motive. I haven't figured that out yet, but we will try to get her to fess up. I need our best interrogator at the Fairfax County Jail as soon as possible. I am standing outside the Capitol Building, freezing my butt off, waiting for Fletcher to pick me up. It will be at least an hour, maybe two before I can get there."

"Okay, I'll get someone there asap."

"Make sure he waits for me to brief him before he tackles her."

"Okay, and Colt, nice job my boy. I knew you would get him, I mean her. I want you to feel free to lead the release of this to the media. We need to get the word out that the killer is in custody. There is a lot of tension and fear out there."

"Yes, sir."

It took two hours to get to the jail in Fairfax. Our best interrogator, Jim Kuntz had arrived just minutes before. Seeing Chuck Ellis in the waiting area, I invited him to meet with us in the conference room. I introduced the two men and began the briefing. According to several of her colleagues, she is highly intelligent, and I can attest that she can be quite feisty, so be careful in there. After going over the evidence we had, which ties her to the murder scene of at least two of the murders, I emphasized that we have no clue as to motive. Jim that will be your job

find that, and I think we can wrap this up very quickly.

Jim said, "Okay, tell them to bring her down, I'll let her stew for a while until I get my thoughts together and develop a plan."

Chuck and I went into the surveillance room and waited for them to bring her in. We watched thru the two-way mirror, as they handcuffed her left hand to a ring on the table in front of her chair. We noticed that she was upset at being cuffed.

When Kuntz stepped into the room, she looked him over very intently, then raised her left arm, shaking it so as to rattle the chain and said, "Is this really necessary."

Jim responded, "Well, Ma'am, I am not with this department, so I'm not familiar with their rules, but since they think you are guilty of multiple murders, I would assume that it is prudent at the very least."

"Oh, so I'm dealing with the FBI, I guess and a smart ass to boot."

"Well, probably not as smart as you from what I've been told, but I'm no slouch at what I do. They would not have sent an incompetent to interview you, this is a very important case to us, and we would like to get it settled as soon as possible."

I had kept my focus on her, not looking at Jim at all. The minute he said I am no slouch at what I do, I saw her countenance change. I thought, "Uh oh, she has taken that as a challenge, be careful Jim." Sure enough, when he asked her to verify certain personal information for the record, she responded, "Don't bother me with that BS, you already know all that." From that point on she clammed up and gave no responses to his questions. He kept at it for about fifteen minutes but got nowhere. Finally, he called out, "Okay, you can take her back to her cell."

I thanked Jim for his effort and told him to go home. We are going to let her sleep on it overnight, and I plan on using a female interrogator tomorrow. After he left, I called Jim Olsen and made arrangements for the female agent to meet me tomorrow at 10 AM. I told him I was going to set up a news conference to take place as soon as I had time to get my remarks in written form. "Do you want me to send you a copy for your approval?"

"No, you know what to say and what not to as well. I'll be watching the late news reports."

I set the wheels rolling for a major news announcement at 10 PM in the Jail conference room and secluded myself to write out my statement.

At exactly 10 PM I gave the following statement: "Good evening, ladies and gentlemen, I am Special Agent, Colt McLean, in charge of the Task Force established to investigate the series of murders of US Congressmen. I am pleased to announce that we have made an arrest in the murder of Congressman Mack Davis and we believe that we will soon be able to charge the same individual with the other murders as well. Tonight, at my direction, Sergeant Charles "Chuck" Ellis arrested Sally Matthews, age 29 and had her transported to the Fairfax County Jail.

"As we began our investigation, one of the first assumptions we made was that the killer had to have been known by the victims and that he or she must have great physical strength as well as an excellent knowledge of scripture, to have left notes found on all the victims. A review of known congressional staff first brought Miss Matthews to our attention. "She is a world-class athlete, and although she is a paraplegic, she has great upper body strength. She is also the daughter of a Baptist Minister, and she is well versed in scripture and quite capable of quoting it. I personally interviewed her, and she gave an accounting of her presence at the office at the time of three of the murders. Later, for reasons I will not go into at this time, her fellow worker recanted her confirmation and admitted that Miss Matthews actually came to the office at least two and maybe three hours later than she first claimed. This afternoon when I confronted Miss Matthews with the fact that her alibi had been proven false, she said, 'Unless you can place me at the murder scenes, and you can't, stop trying to blow smoke up my' (you know what). When she drove off, I discovered the print left in the snow by her chairlift to be an exact match for that found at the Davis farm on the day he was killed. Based on that I ordered her arrest. I will remind you that her van is wired so that the engine will not start unless the wheelchair is securely locked into place behind the steering wheel of the van. It is a reasonable assumption to make that if her van was at the scene, so was she.

"Now, I would like to speak to our viewing audience; you can be of assistance to us as we continue this investigation. Miss Matthews drives a 2016 GMC, blue and white van bearing a Virginia license plate WZX 4875. It is equipped with folding doors on the middle right side of the van, and of course, has a motorized chair lift installed. If anyone can place that van in the following areas on the dates indicated they should call the number scrolling across the screen.

Beaufort County, North Carolina	February 10th
District of Columbia, NW	Morning of February 12th
Brandywine, Maryland	Morning of February 20th
Rockingham County, Virginia	February 25th

"In our interrogation of her earlier this evening, she refused to cooperate and answered only a few of our questions. We will try again tomorrow at 10 o'clock. Until further notice, we will hold a press briefing here at 4 PM each day. If I cannot be here the Sheriff and or his representative will give you as much information as we can. Now I will take your questions."

The next 15 minutes were excruciating for me. The questions were mostly ones that they knew we couldn't or wouldn't answer, and some were explained in my statement, making me wonder if they even listened. I finally made it to my car at about 10:45.

I called Ellen as soon as the engine fired up, "Hello my Prince, I am so proud of you," were her exact words.

"Do you have the news on?"

"Oh yeah, sitting here waiting for it to come on, that is. The 10 o'clock news had a bulleting saying stay tuned for breaking news on the killing of United States Congressman. To be aired at eleven o'clock."

"Look, I see what looks like black ice out here, so I think I will hang up, let you watch the news and I will call you when I get home." It was indeed treacherous driving until I reached the beltway, but I made it home without having an accident.

It was 11:35 by the time we reconnected. She was in awe of seeing her sweetie on national TV but would much rather be holding me in her arms was the general message as I understood it. I told her to get used to it as I had committed to a daily 4 PM press briefing until further notice. It had been a long day, and I was way too tired to journal. I crashed just after midnight.

CHAPTER 13

SATURDAY, MARCH 9TH: Logging unto our system at 7:35 AM, I learned of events that had occurred yesterday at about the same time I was ordering Sally Matthews arrest. It seems that Congressman Farmer had decided to head home to Reston, Virginia, earlier than usual, due to weather conditions. Our agent meant to tail him home but experienced car trouble and lost contact with the congressman. We were unable to get a backup in time to follow Mr. Farmer home.

Someone from Fletchers' Boathouse, located across the river in D.C., notified the Arlington County Police that they saw a car crashing down from the George Washington Memorial Parkway toward the Potomac River. Arlington County Rescue responded to find the congressman dead by the time they were able to reach his car. They thought someone forced his car off that steep cliff but had no definite proof.

I decided to stay with my plan of going directly from my apartment to jail. As I drove toward Fairfax, I thought, "We now have six dead Congressmen, all had been Democrats, with the one defection mentioned earlier. Obviously, the last one wasn't done by the serial killer; she is in jail. I wonder if we will ever know whether the last one was murder or an accident?"

I arrived at the jail just before 10 AM and met Special Agent Jessica Phillips. We talked, and I learned that she was relatively new to our agency, "Been here about two years," was the way she

put it. I told her about our previous session, and how Sally had been determined to show Kuntz, she was as smart as he. "So, do not say anything that she can take as a challenge, just try to get her to open up as to her motive in all this mess. I think you might try to get her to see that we have enough circumstantial evidence to convict her - - maybe that will work."

She asked to see a playback of last night's session with Jim Kuntz. After that, she said, "Give me a few minutes then bring her in."

I went out, to make the arrangements and proceeded to the witness room. From behind the two-way mirror, I watched them bring Sally in. Jessica stood from her position on the far side of the table. When the office started to cuff Sally to the ring on the table, Jessica said, "That won't be necessary, officer." He didn't argue, just turned and exited the room.

Sally spoke up as soon as Jessica took her seat, "I appreciate this," she held up her hand to indicated the decision not to put her in cuffs. "And, I'm glad to see that the FBI has decided to be more civil and to send a woman to do the job. Maybe you will make some progress, let's see."

Jessica said, "Sally, I see that you have not exercised your right to an attorney, do you think that is wise?"

"Here is the way I see it, if I don't talk, I don't need a lawyer, and I have chosen not to talk, sort of wait and see what you guys can come up with before I do so."

"Honey, I have to tell you, we have enough evidence to get a guilty conviction and in my best judgment that will almost definitely mean a death sentence for you. Are you sure you want to go down that road?"

"I don't have any choice, do I."

"Well, if you cooperate, make it easier for us, we could recommend leniency."

"What judge in his right mind would be lenient with a serial killer?"

"Is there anything I can do or say to get you to help us wrap this thing up?"

"No, for you I am almost persuaded but, I think I will stick to my plan to remain silent."

"Then we are wasting our time here, is that right?"

"Yes, I am afraid so."

They said goodbye and Jessica called for the officer to come in and take Sally to her cell. I watched with mixed emotions, proud to see the rapport that almost succeeded in getting her to talk and yet, sad to think, what is it going to take to break her?

Later that afternoon, I got a clue of what it might take when her father called me. I answered my cell phone, and he said, "This is Pastor Ralph Matthews, I am Sally Matthews' father."

"Hello, sir and may I ask how you got my number?"

"Yes, I have been to the jail several times, and they will not let me see my daughter. A Corporal Ellis found me in the waiting area and came over to offer me comfort as I sat there crying. After telling him I thought I could help get her to tell what really happened, he gave me your number."

"If you have information that will help us get the information we need, I am ready to listen."

"Agent McLean, please do not misunderstand that my willingness to help means that I do not love my daughter because I do. I have spent my entire adult life in teaching my children and preaching to my congregations that truth and justice matter. I cannot sit by and let those life principles get covered up because they might negatively impact someone I love."

"I see what you mean."

"I know her quite well, having dealt with her for almost 30 years now, she is brilliant, as I am sure you have discovered. One of her flaws is that she does not manage her anger well and has a tendency to spout off more than she should when she is angry. So, your task will be to make her mad and to keep goading her until she tells you what you need to know. Now, the easiest way to do that is to create a competitive situation between her, and her brothers or even me. Another thing that will get her dander up is the mention of anything to do with the former President."

"I guess I am the man for the job then because I am pretty sure just the sight of me will get her blood pressure up. We have had several semi-explosive encounters already."

"That sounds like a good way to start. But, I need to say a few more things. First, I want you to know that she was not like this before her accident. Oh, she was competitive especially with her brothers, but after the accident, she turned against God, and her competitiveness became an absolute compulsion to win and that has caused a chasm between us all."

"I'm sorry to hear that sir."

"Let me finish. The reason I am doing this is because I serve a God, who loves his people and who can forgive a murderer as easily as he forgives a liar. I want you to promise me that if you get her to confess to the murders, you will grant me a visit of at least an hour with her very soon after that. I need to assure her that I love her and that God also does. It is vitally important that she repent and seek forgiveness, I need to feel that I have been a part of that process. Will you promise me that?"

"Yes sir, I promise."

"Good, then let me tell you what I think must be the root cause behind all this."

I listened for several more minutes and gave him my sincere thanks for his help.

That night as I related all that had gone on today to Ellen, she began to weep. "What's wrong darling," I asked.

"Oh, I just find it so sad and yet heart-warming to hear of a father who loves his daughter enough to let truth prevail and to trust God to take care of her soul."

That almost made me cry. I told her I was thinking about driving down tomorrow to get maybe two or three hours with her before I had to turn around and drive back.

"No way, Colt McLean. You are not going to spend 12 hours on the road, as tired as you are for a few kisses and hugs from me. You stay home and rest. In fact, I don't think you should go to church tomorrow. Sleep as long as you can, and maybe you should watch A Few Good Men on Netflix. That movie has a great courtroom interrogation scene where the lawyer gets the Colonel to confess.

I agreed and did as she had suggested.

CHAPTER 14

EARLY MONDAY MORNING I received a call from Sgt. Dellinger. "We found him, and indeed he was drunk but sober enough to make some sense of what had happened. He did see a woman in a wheelchair get out of a van that he heard coming up the driveway. He witnessed her using the ax and lost his lunch. I have him in the Harrisonburg jail to sober up. What else do you want me to do?"

"Just tell him that I have notified his family and that they will be coming to get him. And let him know that we will not be charging him with any crime, but that he will be needed to testify when the trial occurs."

I immediately dialed his sister and told her that he is incarcerated in Harrisonburg but that he would not face any charges in the matter. She said they would get there today either by car or by air and asked me to let Jimmy know, "We are coming for you."

I did as she asked and then decided to go directly to the Fairfax County Jail via the beltway rather than go to my office. I had prepared my daily report on Sunday afternoon, and so, I forwarded it to Olsen and checked the system before I left my apartment. I waited until 9 PM hoping the traffic would be somewhat lighter, and it turned out to be a good move, as I arrived in just over 30 minutes.

When Sally entered the room and saw me there, her eyes

squinted, and her hatred for me raged onto her countenance. I waited for the deputy to cuff her to the table and leave. She blurted out, "So, back to the hairy leg variety and the cruel and unusual treatment, I see."

"Oh, Sally, I am just following protocol, I would never be cruel to you. In fact, this is more of a social call than an interrogation session. I want to see if you are being treated well and to deliver some messages to you from your family."

"You are not fooling me, you don't give a crap how I am treated, and I don't give a crap about messages from my family. But, if you really do care, order me a foam mattress for my cot, that two-inch piece of crap I have is awful."

"Sorry, I can't help you with that, but I thought you might want to know how your brothers responded to my question about whether you could have committed these murders." I reached in my inner suit pocket, pulled out my notebook, and said, "Let me get this straight, it was David that said, 'Yeah, she might have done it, if they pissed her off, she is certainly capable of doing it.' It was Henry who said, 'No way, she doesn't have the balls for that kind of thing.'"

"What the hell does Hank Matthews know about anything. You tell him that I may not have the physical ones, but I've got more stones than he and David combined. I told you once before, McLean, I can do anything anyone else can do, except walk."

"I will tell him what you said. Oh, I almost forgot, he also told me you voted for Barack Obama the first time he ran, is that true?"

"Damn him; he never gets tired of throwing that in my face. I did because I believed he deserved the chance to be the first black president. What a freaking mistake that was, history will not treat that man well."

"What is it with you two? Is he deliberately trying to get under your skin? He said, 'Be sure and tell her, if she did it, I hope she winds up in the same cell block with the last Democratic candidate she voted for.'"

With that, she became extremely agitated, and her voice raised several decibels when she almost yelled, "That really pisses me off, she deserved the chance to be the first woman president. You men have screwed up this country for over 240 years. It was time for a woman to show everyone what she could do. She was supposed to win. It's not fair." With that, she began to slam both fists on the table repeatedly and started to cry.

I waited a few seconds and then asked, "Well why didn't she win?" "Because of people like those five bastards. Do you realize that none of them voted to support their own party's candidate for President?"

"So, that's why you killed them!"

"You're damn right it is!"

I remained silent and waited for her crying to subside and watched as it slowly dawned on her what she had just done. It was almost a full minute before she raised her head from the table and asked, "Did I just confess to murdering those five congressmen?"

"Yes, my dear, you did."

"Well, I guess I'm a little late, but I definitely need a lawyer, so if you don't mind, go ahead and ask a judge to appoint one for me."

"I'll do that."

"You're a real prick, you know."

"I've been told that before. By the way, now that you have confessed to having done the deed, why don't you tell me how you got Mack Davis on that fence?"

"Hey, it wasn't all that hard. When Mack invited me to meet General Sherman, I came up behind him and used my hydraulic device to stand. When I hit him with the blackjack, he fell back into my arms. I simply lowered him into my lap and backed away from the horse. It was while I was putting away the blackjack that his head slipped off to the side and his blood got on the floor."

"So, you took him to the fence in your wheelchair and then I guess you used the hydraulic device to stand you both up to the fence."

"You are not as dumb as you look, McLean. All I had to do was turn him around and hook the hoodie over the fence. The rest was relatively easy, I went back to the van and got the scimitar, that I had bought at a garage sale one Saturday morning about a month before. Luckily, I had wrapped it in an old tablecloth, actually made of oilcloth, because that kept me from getting his blood on myself or the wheelchair. The hardest part was deciding how to use the scimitar; it's a good thing I had anatomy courses in my pre-med days before the accident."

I thanked her for clearing up how she got him on the fence, told her that I was going to make arrangements for her father to visit her and called for the guard to take her back to her cell. Before the guard came in, I told her that we had an eyewitness to the murder of Congressman Martinez. That really shocked her, but she asked no questions. So, I said nothing further and just let him take her back to her cell.

Then I went out and ordered several DVDs of the video session, set up the visit by her father, emphasizing that they are to be allowed to be together, and arranged for a press briefing for 11:30. That provided about an hour and a half for the press to assemble, which should be sufficient time. During the next few minutes, I called Reverend Matthews and expressed my sympathy as I delivered the news that Sally had confessed to murdering all five of the men. He began to sob but was thankful when I told him that he could come and visit her at any time. I did warn him that the press would be all over the place in about an hour. The next calls were to Olsen and Ellen. Then I prepared for the press briefing.

At exactly 11: 30, I started the briefing to a packed room.

After introducing myself, I began with the statement: I believe most of you are aware that on two previous interrogation sessions with Sally Matthews, we were unsuccessful in learning her motive for the murder of Congressman Davis or any of the other four men. This morning, based on tips provided by someone very close to Sally, I was able to obtain the information we needed to proceed with charging her with all five of the murders.

If you recall, in our previous briefing, we indicated that the motive behind these killings had to be something, other than the obvious, and probably involved something the killer knew about these men that we do not know. As it turned out, she is a feminist who is extremely distraught that we did not elect our first female President of the United States. As I had been advised to do, I used her anger over this issue, to find out that she believed that none of these democratic congressmen, voted for their party candidate in the last Presidential Election. When asked if that was why she killed them, she responded, and I quote, "You're damn right it is!" Based on her confession we will be charging her with murdering all five of them.

I will now take a few questions before I have to leave to take care of these matters.

The first question was, do you know how she knew how they voted?

"No, we do know that she met with all them during the month of November 2017, which was a year after the election. Nor do we know if the information she had was accurate or not. We think that to be immaterial to the case. She thought she knew how they voted and she acted on that."

Next, someone asked if there is any evidence that she might have intended to go after anyone else?

"No there is no such evidence. We know that she was tasked with polling all Democrats in Congress to determine if they would support the pending tax relief legislation. And we know that only these five members agreed to meet with her. So, now that she is in jail, I assume that all congressmen and women can feel safe, even those Democrats who might not have voted for their party nominee."

I cut the questions off soon after that and proceeded down the hall to find Reverend Matthews, whom I had seen entering the building just before the briefing. As I was inquiring about his presence, I saw him coming into the reception area. He saw me at the same instant, and we walked quickly to meet each other. He held out his hand, we shook, and he collapsed our arms to give me a half hug. As he backed off, I saw the tears flowing down his cheeks, and his chin and lower lip were quivering preventing him from speaking. Finally, he held his hands in the air, in the Christian tradition meaning Praise the Lord, and he said, "She - -, she let me hold her." And I knew the tears were tears of joy. "The first time in five years - - five years, how sweet it was."

I felt my own tears flow down my cheeks, "I am so glad for you Reverend. Were you able to achieve your objective?"

"Yes, no, - - oh, I don't know. I do know that I convinced her that no matter what she had done, she is still my baby and I love her. I think I convinced her that God feels the same way. She did agree that it was her that moved away from God and not the other way around, and with that, I believe she can move back toward him. She did promise me that she would get back into the Word of God, so, I left her a copy of the New Testament provided by Gideon's International."

After saying goodbye to the Reverend, I picked up the three copies of the videoed interrogation session, I had previously ordered and made it to Olsen's office as fast as I could. When I walked in, Jeanette ran from behind her desk to give me a big hug and to congratulate me. I handed her one of the DVD's and told her you can watch this on your computer before you enter into evidence. "Can I go in?"

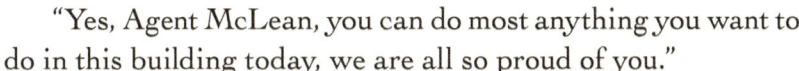

"Yes, Agent McLean, you can do most anything you want to do in this building today, we are all so proud of you."

I knocked. "Enter."

He jumped up and came to greet me with a big handshake. "Nice work, Colt. Now, tell me that you have a video of that interrogation scene for me to watch."

"I do," and I reached into my coat pocket and pulled out the two DVD's I had left. "This one is for your personal use, and this one is mine," I said, as I handed one to him and slipped the other into my inside coat pocket. "Jeanette has the other copy I had made, and she will enter it into the evidence file as soon as she finishes watching it.

He hurried to his computer, popped the DVD in and motioned me to sit in the chair beside his desk. When it was over, he turned to me and said, "That was fantastic, how in the world did you do that? Maybe we should make you our top interrogator."

"I had a lot of help, help that I don't want too many people to know about, at least for a while. Her father called me Saturday and told me that when angered, she tends to blurt out what is on her mind. He, even gave me hints on how to prod her into anger, using the competitiveness of her and her brothers. He also told me that he thought her motive must have something to do with the last Presidential Election. I simply took his information and ran with it."

"Well, it was masterfully done. I know the Director will want to see you tomorrow, so, wear your best suit. I call you in the morning when I know his schedule."

Back at my office in Crystal City, I found everyone in a festive mood. Someone had gone to a nearby grocery store and purchased several bottles of cheap champagne, and when I walked in, they began to sing, For He's a Jolly Good Fellow. That was the first time that had ever happened to me, and I must admit it capped off a very nice day.

That night, I related the entire day's activities to Ellen, and I told her, "You know, this has been a special day, and I will always be proud of getting her to confess. But maybe the most memorable event of the day was seeing the joy Reverend Matthews felt when he told me he had got to hold his daughter for the first time in five years. I cried unashamedly." I heard her sniffling and knew she was reaching for the ever-present tissue box, to get a tissue and wipe away her own tears.

CHAPTER 15

———◦◆◦———

TUESDAY, MARCH 13ᵀᴴ. I dressed in my best suit and paid close attention to my personal grooming, hey, I'm not stupid. Even though I had met the Director of the FBI on one other occasion, this was to be special. At my office, Olsen told me to arrive at his office by 9:45 as we had a 10:00 meeting with the Director. I was Johnny on the spot.

The Director was very gracious with his compliments on my performance as head of the Task Force and indicated that I had a great future in the organization. After that, he stood and said, "Gentlemen, if you will leave your weapons on my desk, we are going to be taking a short ride, and we will not be allowed firearms, where we are going. Follow me."

We arrived at the back gate of the White House, just a few minutes later and entered on the side of the building facing the Executive Office Building. There was an escort waiting who took us to the elevator where we went upstairs to the Oval Office, where we were ushered right into that grand and historical office. The President of the United States was standing in front of his desk with a huge smile on his face. "Come in gentlemen; I am pleased that you are here." He shook hands with the three of us and said to the Director, "Thanks for letting me view yesterday's interrogation." Turning to me he gave a hearty handshake and patted me on the chest with his free hand and said, "Colt that was a marvelous piece of work." Then he invited us all to sit on the couches arranged at the other end of the room. He took a wingback chair in the center and said, "I just wanted to take a few minutes to share with all of you my appreciation for the excellent work you have done to bring this serial killer to justice in such a short time. Keeping America safe is my primary objective, and I can only do so much with policies and the use of Executive Orders, it is really you all and our military and other law enforcement officials who do the real work. I just want you to get the credit you deserve."

I was so in awe my mouth gaped open. At the same time, the President must have noticed that I was surprised to see a cameraman taking pictures from all angles, because he said, "There is a requirement that a pictorial history be made of all visitors to this office. Don't worry we will see that you get sufficient copies for your personal needs."

I think we all thanked him at the same time.

I finally got up the courage to say, "Sir, I cannot tell you how much this means to me, I never in my wildest dreams thought I would have the opportunity to be in this great place and to have the President of the United States saying thank you to me a lowly civil servant. I am blown away." As I was talking I let my eyes roam around the room and I must have paused when I saw the bust of Martin Luther King Jr., because the president said, "That bust has been right there all the time. I will tell you that." He stood, and said, "Gentlemen, I do appreciate you coming, but I do have a heavy schedule that demands my attention."

We rose, and he shook each of our hands again. He told the Director, "I know I can count on you to ensure that Colt receives the highest rewards possible for his fine work." I was the last one, and he said to me, "Colt, is there any chance you would consider coming to work for the Secret Service? We could use a man like you here in the White House."

"Sir, that is a great compliment. I am pleased beyond words that you would consider having me, but I have plans for the near future that I have not even discussed with my boss here, so I will gratefully decline."

One the way back to the Hoover Building, I exclaimed, "Wow! What an experience. I keep pinching myself to make sure I am not dreaming. To think that the president would take time from his busy schedule to say thank you to us, it is so - - fantastic - - incredible."

Olsen chimed in, "Yes it was, I certainly never thought that I would get to enter that room." The Director just smiled, I'm sure because he had been there on numerous occasions.

After retrieving our weapons, we made it made to Jim's office, where he said, "I think you have something to discuss with me.?"

"Yes, I do, and if you do not object, I would like to invite Jeanette in also. She has been a real friend to me over the years. No need to tell this twice."

We walked in, and he asked Jeanette too, "Join us in my office, please."

After the three of us were seated, I said, "There are two new passions in my life, which I have not shared with either of you. I need to do that now. First, I have met someone, and I am so in love. I feel like a teenager, and I intend to ask her to marry me. I will do that tonight, and I am quite confident that her answer will be yes. She has previously indicated that if we were to become committed to each other that she would follow me wherever I wanted us to live. But I am convinced that she will be happier if she stays where she has always lived, in Washington, North Carolina. Therefore, I am going to resign from the FBI and go to her and try to make her as happy as I possibly can. I can best pursue my second passion from there as well."

Jeanette reached over and took my right hand and brought the back of it to her cheek and said, "Oh Colt, I am so glad that you have found someone to love. You cannot go wrong by doing everything you can to make your life mate happy."

Olsen said, "I am in shock. Here you are at the top of your career, having been assured that your future is secure, met with the President of the United States, and you are going to walk away from all this?"

"Yes, I am, because of my other passion, about which I want to tell you. As I worked these five murder cases, it necessitated my involvement in the political arena more than ever before. What I found has alarmed me to such a degree that I honestly believe our democracy stands on a precipice over which it must not fall. There is a danger out there far more significant than a serial killer, a threat that is being orchestrated by some very evil people, with the intent of destroying America. My passion is to write a book that will hopefully wake up America to this threat."

We talked on for several minutes, and I could tell that Jeanette had something on her mind that she was not willing to share in this setting. Olsen finally said, "Colt, I'm not sure what to say, on the one hand, I can thank you for your service here and wish you to best with your book. On the other hand, I can't help but feel that you are missing out on a great career by not staying with us."

We shook hands, and I said, "I owe you both a great deal of gratitude, please know that I treasure you both. But, my mind is made up, and when I walk out of here, I am heading to Human Resources to discuss my options for the future. I thank you both from the bottom of my heart."

Jeanette grabbed my hand, and we walked out together. In the outer office, she squeezed my hand and said, "I am so pleased that you are following your passions, life is just too short not to do so. I have an idea that I would like you to consider. My husband's nephew is a reporter for the Washington Post. I think we can persuade him to do an article about you that will be good publicity for you coming book. You need to take advantage of your current popularity, I mean you have had national television coverage almost every night this past week, a story in the Post

should whet the publics' appetite for your book. What do you think?"

"Why, I think that would be great. I would appreciate anything you can do to make that happen."

At the HR office, I was counseled as to my options and assured that my Civil Service Retirement System funds could be transferred to a self-directed IRA account or left in place until I decided to rejoin the workforce with another law enforcement agency. I thanked her and made arrangements for my resignation to take place tomorrow, at which time I would turn in all federal property in my possession, i.e., car, lap-top, firearm, etc.

Back at the office in Crystal City, I called everyone into the conference room and gave them the news. The retelling of the visit to the Oval Office was received with loud cheers, my decision to resign from the FBI with gasps of unbelief. I gave them the same basic info that I had told Jim Olsen and let them know that tomorrow would be my last day at work and that I hoped to be moving to North Carolina by Sunday.

CHAPTER 16

---◆◇◆---

WHEN I CALLED Ellen at about 7 PM, she answered with, "Hello Prince Charming, am I going to get to see you on national news tonight?"

"You just might, I don't know if it will make the news, but I had a pretty awesome day. Yours truly was invited to the White House, where the Director of the FBI, my boss James Olsen and I met with the President in the Oval Office. Now whether that will get national coverage, I don't know, but I can tell you it was really special for me. He shook my hand, patted me on the chest and even offered me a job with the Secret Service, working at the White House."

"Wow! That is awesome. Did you accept the offer?"

"No, I turned it down, I thanked him for the offer and told him I had other plans."

"What plans?"

"I will tell you in a few minutes, but first, I need to switch roles from Prince Charming to Mr. Practicality."

"Oh, have I heard from him before?"

"Yes, at least on one occasion. You knew you weren't talking to Mr. Romantic, but you didn't actually identify Mr. Practicality."

"Okay, Mr. Practicality, what do you have to say for yourself?"

"Ellen Buck, I love you, and I want to spend the rest of my

life with you, and I will try my best every day to make you happy. Will you please marry me?"

There was a pause, and I hear the tissue box rattle, as she quickly grabbed a tissue. She finally choked out, "Yes Colt McLean, I will gladly marry you. When?"

"What else can Mr. Practicality say but right away. How about Monday afternoon or evening?"

"Seriously, do you have a place up there for us to live?"

"No. I don't want us to live up here. I will be arriving Sunday afternoon with my stuff in a U-Haul van."

"You are going to live here, with me. I get Prince Charming plus I get to stay here in the place I love. Oh, Colt, that will be wonderful."

"Actually, you get Prince Charming, Mr. Practicality, a work in progress Mr. Romantic as well as a soon to be world class writer of the best-selling book of the decade. I will be resigning from the FBI tomorrow and doing my best to close up things here and be there by Sunday."

"You are quitting your job to become a writer. What if that doesn't work out or what if the position here does not get funded again? I guess we can live off my salary ... I interrupted, "I may have forgotten to mention that when I sold the orchard to a builder, I invested that money, it now has a six-figure value, and we could live off the dividend income if we need to."

"Well, you almost had me thinking that you wanted to be a kept man and now I find out that I am to be half owner of a six-figure investment account. Not a bad day's work, if I do say so myself."

We laughed at that, and then I asked, "Do you think you could stand getting rid of that early American, 1960's looking stuff in the sunroom and let me furnish that one room with my stuff?"

"Yes, I will have the Salvation Army come get it before you get here. What are you bringing?"

"I have a brown leather couch and matching recliner, a nice desk, a floor lamp, a computer-stand and two small bookshelves. Other than those things, it will be just my clothes, personal items and maybe a few books. I am going to be taking a lot of stuff to the Salvation Army by Thursday."

"I think those things will fit very nicely in that room. Oh, I am so excited, I'm afraid that I might pee my pants."

"Ellen put the phone down and go; I'll hang on until you get back."

A few minutes later, I hear, "I'm back."

"Okay, Mr. Practicality speaking again, how about this for a plan. Monday morning, I will walk down to the jewelry store, and if that ring we saw before is still there, I will try to make a deal to get it for you. We can get to the Court House before noon and get the license. Do you think you can get Pastor Carey to marry us sometime Monday afternoon or night?"

"I like the plan. You know, I think it would be nice to get married in the conference room at the Sheriff's office. What do you think of that idea?"

"Suits me. We just need to set a time when BJ and the kids, and maybe Joe and Tilly can be there. Now, if you can get the rest of the week off, I will set up a short honeymoon at Atlantic Beach and promise you a better one when I finish writing the book."

We agreed on the plan and called it a night with our usual kiss, kiss sounds.

The rest of the week flew by. Wednesday, I went to Best Buy and purchased a new laptop computer and cell phone. Returned to the apartment to download the things I wanted to keep from the government-owned devices to my new ones and then went to the Hoover Building. There I turned in all my government owned things, signed the required paperwork stating that I voluntarily resigned my position with the FBI and got Mark Fletcher to drive me back to Crystal City. After cleaning out my desk and boxing up my personal items, I made the rounds to say goodbye to all the people with whom I worked. It felt really weird walking the two blocks down the street to the U-Haul rental place to pick up my prearranged truck, with a box on my shoulder. I got over it quick enough.

That afternoon I began the process of going through everything I had accumulated over the years and started making two separate stacks, one for the dumpster, and one for the Salvation Army. Around 4 o'clock Jeanette called to tell me that the reporter for the Post, her nephew named Andy Brown, wanted to come by early tomorrow on his way to the office, to interview me for the story. With that out of the way, she said, "Colt, they have set up a very special going away party for you for Friday noon at the Fort Myer Officer's Club. The Director will be there to present you a special award. So, dress your best, the Post photographer will also be there to get your picture for the article that Andy hopes to get in the Saturday morning issue."

After ending that call, I started carrying junk out back to the dumpster and within an hour that stack was depleted. At 6:30 Mark Fletcher showed up to help me start loading the things that I would donate to the Salvation Army into the truck. As we were loading my bed and other bedroom furniture, Mark commented, "I guess you will be sleeping on the couch tonight."

"Yes, and that big old thing is quite comfortable, I'll have you know. I have fallen asleep on it many times and started a new day as comfortable as if I had been in my own bed." When we finished loading, I treated him to the delicious Chinese buffet at the Golden China as my way of thanking him for his help. I was one tired puppy when I hit the couch that night.

Thursday, March 15th: I must have been super tired because I had a good night's sleep, even if it was on the couch, and awoke over an hour later than usual. I had finished breakfast and brushed my teeth when the doorbell rang. It was Andy Brown, as I had expected. What I had not expected was a man who was probably in his late twenties and who had a tan that looked like he had just come from the beach. He saw my reaction and said, "Hey, I just got back from a week of water skiing in the Caribbean, that's my passion, what can I say."

"Come in, hey you look great, I just wasn't expecting the tan. So, you are Jeanette's nephew. I want you to know that she is a very special person in my book."

"Thanks, I can say the same. Look, let's get right down to it, you made the news down there too, so, between the news stories and Aunt Jeanette's input, I have a good feel for the background of the story I want to write. What I need is for you to fill me in on why you are resigning from the FBI, and what you are going to be doing. It will be hard to meet the deadline for Saturday morning's issue, but I will try. Hopefully, I will be able to get you an advance copy for your editorial review. No guarantee, you understand?"

He sat on the couch and pulled a stenographer's notepad out of his satchel, took out two pens, and said, "I'm ready whenever you are." I took a seat in the recliner and began to relate to him my two passions. It took about twenty minutes, and he was on his way. I headed for the truck to deliver what Mark and I had loaded the night before. After dropping all that off at the Salvation Army, I made the rounds to several grocery stores collecting boxes and headed to the apartment for a boring days' work. Mark and I had dumped contents from dresser drawers in heaps on the bedroom floor; I started there. I determined to keep only the best of my underwear, socks, and other miscellaneous items, folded the ones to keep and boxed them up. The rest went into large plastic bags again sorted into a group to donate and one to go to the dumpster. Then on to the kitchen, where I kept only my mother's silver service and a couple of boxes of non-perishable items from the pantry. I tackled my closet next with the same determination. By late afternoon, I was amazed at how many things I had to again deliver to the Salvation Army. But, before doing that, I surveyed the items that would be loaded for the trip to North Carolina and then proceeded to the truck to visualize the loading of those things on Sunday morning. Next, I delivered the rest of the items to the Salvation Army and went to the hardware store where I purchased bungee cords of various lengths, fifty feet of small-sized rope, and an extendable aluminum rod on which to hang my good clothes. It was a satisfying day's work.

Friday, March 16th: It felt weird driving into the parking lot of the prestigious Officer's Club on Fort Myer in Arlington, in a U-Haul truck, but hey, that's the only transportation I have at the moment. I found my goodbye party's location on the marquee and took the elevator up to the next floor. I walked into a room filled with about 50 people. Jeanette rushed to embrace me and then escorted me around the room to greet the guests. They had a head table set up with the Director in the center, me on his right, Jim Olsen on his left and Jeanette on my right. The meal was excellent, prime rib with crispy onion strings, mashed potatoes and gravy, steamed asparagus and a huge slice of carrot cake for dessert.

After the meal, the Director asked me to follow him to the table at the center of the room on the far left, where there were several items on a table, some of them draped with a cloth to await the right time to be unveiled. He took the mic and gave a very complimentary speech, thanking me for my fifteen years of service and wishing me well in my future endeavors. He turned back toward the table and said, "But before you go we have several gifts for you, well actually, this first one is not a gift. It is something that you earned, and it gives me a great deal of pleasure to present you the Department's most prestigious award." He picked up a blue folder with the FBI shield embossed in Gold on the front, opened it and read a citation that made me sound like one of the Super Hero's from the comic books.

He then pinned the FBI Medal for Meritorious Achievements to my lapel and gently turned me toward the cameraman who came forward to take our picture. "Now, for the gifts," he said as he picked up a large photograph of the Hoover Building. The matt framing the photo had signatures and short messages all around it. "As soon as we are sure everyone here has signed this we will put it back in its' frame and have it ready for you when you leave." He removed the cloth covering two additional photographs, holding up the first one so all could see, as he told them of our visit to the Oval Office. He presented me the picture of the President shaking my hand and patting me on the chest. The picture had been matted and framed, and it contained the bold signature of the President on the matt. The other picture was of the four of us, the President sitting in the wingback chair and the three of us on the two couches. It was beautifully matted and framed also.

"Last and certainly not the least, I have a personal message for you from the President, he requested that you not open it here, but wait until you can open it with your bride." The envelope was marked in the upper left-hand corner in blue ink, The White House, and was hand addressed to Colt and Ellen McLean, in what looked to be the President's handwriting. It was sealed with a gold Presidential Seal with two short blue ribbons attached. I put the envelope in the inside breast pocket of my coat, thanked the Director and took the mic he offered me.

"Friends, I am so thankful that you came to say your goodbyes and I do want to ask all of you to make sure you sign the picture of the Hoover Building before you leave. It, along with these other treasures will have a special place of honor in my new home in North Carolina. These past few weeks have been quite a ride, indeed capping off a career that I once thought rather mundane. Boy, did that change. This past week has been the most incredible week of my life. Some would say, Colt, you have to be the luckiest man alive, and they may be at least partially right. I would say, that I absolutely believe that there was Devine intervention involved. I know I have been blessed to have His support and that of all of you. So, please accept my appreciation for all you have done over these years to help me achieve the success that has come my way. I am without a doubt, blown away. To be in the national limelight for several days running and then to have the President recognize your contributions is almost beyond my comprehension. Today, I found out that the Washington Post will run an article in Saturday's issue telling all about my decision to leave the FBI and to write a story that I believe needs telling. Since all of you will have the opportunity to read that article, I will not bore you with the details here today. Jim Olsen said to me the other day, 'How can you walk away from all this?' The answer is with a little bit of trepidation and a great deal of confidence that I am doing the right thing. Again, I say thank you to you all and may God bless all of you."

Saturday was spent doing last minute things like turning in my 30-day notice to vacate the apartment, going to the post office to have mail forwarded and giving the apartment a thorough cleaning. I was so busy I almost forgot about the article that was supposed to appear in today's Washington Post. I made a quick trip to the drug store, checked to find the article on the front of the local section, and bought three copies. I read it as soon as I got back to the apartment and was quite pleased.

The headline read: Special Agent Colt McLean resigns from the FBI. Colt McLean is perhaps a household name to many of you; certainly, he is here in Washington, D.C. and the surrounding area. For those of you who may have missed his almost nightly appearances on the evening news, he was in charge of the Task Force investigating the series of killings of Democratic Congressmen. He was instrumental in identifying the killer, and he was directly responsible for obtaining her

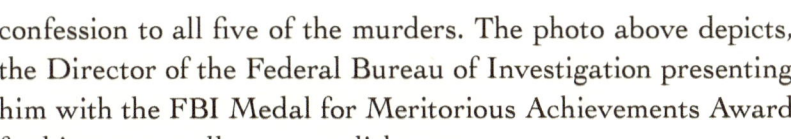

confession to all five of the murders. The photo above depicts, the Director of the Federal Bureau of Investigation presenting him with the FBI Medal for Meritorious Achievements Award for his recent stellar accomplishments.

He accepted this award at his going away party yesterday, along with two beautifully matted and framed photographs taken in the Oval Office where the President of the United States invited him to show his personal appreciation for the wonderful work that he had done.

His boss, Agent James Olsen, the head of the Counter-Intelligence Division, asked him, 'How can you walk away from all this?' Yesterday he responded, 'With a little bit of trepidation and a great deal of confidence.'

I was privileged in interviewing Colt, in order to write this article and I understand why he is proceeding with confidence. I learned that he will be moving to Washington, North Carolina this weekend and will marry his sweetheart, Miss. Ellen Buck on Monday. He plans to make his home there, where 'I believe she will be the happiest she can be.' He also revealed a passion that he admitted came to him while he was investigating these recent murders. Following is a summary of his comments about this new-found passion: Investigating these murders caused me to look more closely than ever before at the political arena in which we find ourselves. I discovered some very alarming things. Things that I believe have the potential to bring our democracy to its knees. I don't know if anyone can change the course the country is traveling, but I feel compelled to try. I plan to write a book using these five murders as the base of the story, which I will entitle Killing Congress, but the book will end with the dangers we are facing as a Nation. And I honestly believe that if we do not correct, the path on which we are now going my story may have to retitled to Killing America.

I wish you well Colt and I will be one of the first in line to buy your new book.

The by-line: Andy Brown.

Sunday morning, Mark came over early, so as to finish in time to drive to Sterling, Virginia to attend his father's church. He seldom misses a Sunday service, especially when his father preaches. We were finished loading by 9 AM and I made it on the road within minutes thereafter.

CHAPTER 17

S EVEN HOURS LATER I pulled the truck into the backyard of my new home on 2nd Street. Beep, beep, I jumped out to greet my fiancée who almost knocked me down as she jumped into my arms. We had barely gotten in a couple of kisses before I heard the roar of an engine coming up behind me. Knowing it was the Edwards clan, I continued the kiss. Beep, beep, "Hey, stop that there are kids present."

We turned in time to catch a twin each, both of whom were grinning from ear to ear. JJ said, "I caught a three-pound bass yesterday."

"All by yourself?"

"Well, daddy helped a little bit, but I caught it."

"Good job, little man. Now let me get a look at little Miss. Tilly. Oh, you precious looking little redhead. Daddy is going to have to get a big stick to beat the boys away from your door, sweetie." Looking into BJ's beaming face, I asked, "And how is little momma doing?"

"Oh, I'm in hog's heaven, it is so nice to have a little one to fuss over day - - and night."

I looked over to see Brody rolling his eyes at that remark. We all laughed.

It was 6 o'clock by the time Brody and I finished unloading the truck, placing the furniture in the sunroom and putting my personal things upstairs. I was pleased that Ellen had rearranged her things to make room in the closet for my clothes and had emptied several drawers for me to use. I was even more surprised to find when I came back downstairs that she and Brody had already hung my pictures in the sunroom. The one of the Hoover building was on the wall over my computer stand and the two taken in the Oval Office were arranged over the couch. I liked what I saw and said so. She responded, "I am going to have the Washington Post article framed and matted to go over there behind your recliner."

"Nice!"

Brody said, "Well, we need to get these kids home and in the tub." He shook my hand and said, "It is really nice to have you here, buddy." As they got into the Escalade, he said to Ellen, "I'll see you in the morning."

"No, you will not Brody Edwards, you gave me the week off, remember."

"Oh, that's right you do have something special planned for tomorrow. Alright, I remember, see you both around 3 o'clock.

After they left, we went back in, and I fell into the recliner fully realizing how tired I was. Ellen came and sat in my lap, and we both rested for almost 30 minutes before she asked, "Are you hungry?"

"Yes, I am. How about you follow me to turn that truck in, and we stop by some fast food place for a quick bite?"

"Okay by me." And off we went.

Monday morning, I awoke at my usual time, quietly got ready, tiptoed past her bedroom door and had coffee brewing and my computer hooked up to her wi-fi network by the time she made it downstairs.

"Good morning, Mr. Practicality."

I grabbed her, pulling her into a crushing embrace and planted a kiss on her intended to impart all my pent-up feelings and emotions. It must have succeeded because she said, "Maybe I should restate that. Good morning, Mr. Romantic."

After breakfast, we walked down to Main Street and proceeded to Stewarts' Jewelry Store where we had window shopped a few weeks earlier. The diamond that had caught our attention was still displayed, so we went in and asked to take a closer look at it. He brought it out of the window, placed it on the counter in front of us, then took a cloth to extract it from the box, wiped it good, and asked Ellen to "Hold out your ring finger." He slipped it on her finger, and it was a perfect fit. As she twisted her hand to admire the sparkling gem, he said, "I have had that one longer than I wanted too, and since I've known Ellen since she was in high school, I will knock off a thousand dollars from the price quoted in the window."

"Do you like it, honey?"

"Oh, yes I like it, but that is an awful lot of money."

Then I remembered something Gene Wilson had told me about his hobby of buying antique jewelry so, I excused myself for just a minute and walked out front to dial his number. When I explained why I was calling, he said, "I'll be glad to help you. Go back inside and ask to see the GIA Independent Grading Report and read it to me. I did that, and then he asked, "How much is he asking for it?" When I told him, he responded, "Buy it! That is an excellent price." I thanked him, hung up.

"We will take it assuming you have a matching wedding band."

"I do, and what about a band for you?"

"We need that also," I said. I tried on several, and we finally selected one that we both liked. I wrote the man a check and hustled her to the Court House. When we walked up to the counter, Ellen took another look at her new treasure, and the lady said, "Well, I bet someone wants to apply for a wedding license."

"You bet, we do. In fact, the wedding is this afternoon."

She said, "No need letting grass grow under your feet, right?"

"Absolutely," I replied. We filled out the paperwork, paid the fee, waited for the lady to fill out the license and then made it back home for lunch. After a BLT sandwich and chips washed down with a glass of sweet tea, Ellen said, "Prince Charming, you need to go up to your temporary quarters and rest, I will wake you in time to get to the station on time."

"What, do you think I'm a kid or something that I need a nap?"

"No, I just think you aren't going to get much sleep tonight."

"Oh, I see." I didn't argue with the woman.

At 2:15 she yelled, "Colt, it's time to wake up."

I had been in a deep sleep, and it took me a few seconds to orient myself. I yelled back, "Can I come over and get my things from the closet?"

"Yes, just let me close the bathroom door. And hurry up, I need to get dressed."

I gathered the things I needed and tried not to gawk at the things she had laid out on the bed that I knew she would soon be wearing. I thought, but had sense enough not to say, those pretty things she had bought are really skimpy, but they sure are pretty. I slammed the door so she would know I was out of there and went to get ready.

Last night, when we talked about the short honeymoon I had planned for Atlantic Beach, she made it clear that she was not willing to wait the hour and a half it would take to get down there. So, I had canceled the first night's stay, and we devised a plan to drive away from the station in the direction of the beach but to double back and spend the first night in her bed. We arrived at the station at 3:30 to find BJ busily decorating the conference room with helium-filled blue and white balloons and matching streamers. There was a cake on a side table with three bottles of Champaign on ice. Tilly was sleeping away in her car seat in a chair in the corner. Ellen asked, "Where are the twins?"

"I imagine JJ is in with the Sheriff and Hannah probably

has her daddy cow-towing to her demands if I know those two." Sure enough, that's where I found them.

Joe and Tilly Cooke arrived at the same time as did Pastor Mark Carey. It was also apparent that several Deputy Sheriff's had come in from patrol to witness the event. The ceremony only lasted a few minutes, it went without hitch, with both of us able to repeat our vows on cue. We exchanged wedding bands and were pronounced man and wife.

The reception was excellent, the cake quite good and there were several presents, produced from beneath the table. BJ offered to drop them by Ellen's on the way home, but Ellen rejected that by saying, "Oh no, that won't be necessary, I just remembered something I forgot to put in the car. We will drop them off before we leave for the beach."

"Quick thinking my dear," I muttered as we pulled out of the parking lot.

"I'm not about to let anyone mess up this night," she said.

I pulled around back, we unloaded the presents, and she instructed me to put the car in the detached garage and get your buns back in this house quick.

We have chosen to let the lyrics to a song tell you all you need to know about the rest of that night.

> And when we get behind closed doors
> Then she lets her hair hang down
> And she makes me glad that I'm a man
> Oh, no one knows what goes on behind closed doors
> Behind closed doors

CHAPTER 18

---◆---

T HE NEXT MORNING just before leaving for the beach and as we opened the wedding presents we had brought home last night, I remembered the envelope from the President. It was still in my coat pocket, so I darted up the steps to retrieve it. Opening it together, we were both amazed to see a hand-written note wishing us a happy marriage from him and the First Lady. It also included a check of a very generous amount which we decided not to disclose to anyone in order to respect his privacy. The note and the picture I took of the check will be a part of our family history for years to come.

Our honeymoon at Atlantic Beach was, what can I say? Fantastic, awesome, beautiful, all of those and then some. I can't express my full range of feelings. Standing on a balcony looking down on the dunes, with the beach just a few yards from you. Watching dolphins bobbing up and down as they pass you by. Viewing a lighthouse visible to the naked eye but even more impressive with binoculars, eating the most delicious seafood one can imagine. It just doesn't get any better than this. And I haven't even mentioned being in the arms of the one you love more than life itself. Wow!

Morning and evening walks along the beach, visiting Fort Macon State Park, strolling thru historic houses in the old sea town of Beaufort, maritime museums, touring the chocolate factory, and oh, an afternoon excursion on a sailboat to get an even better look at the lighthouse on Harker's Island. Seeing the wild ponies grazing on the outer banks. Some of the days are now warm enough to sunbathe, usually tucked up close to the dunes for protection from the wind. Aah - - we enjoyed it all, but as has been said many times, all good things must come to an end.

We checked out from A Place at the Beach at the prescribed time of 11 AM, took a final drive South down the outer banks to take one more look at the bridge to Swansboro, turned back to go into Morehead City for one more seafood lunch and then headed home. On the way, my phone rings and I am surprised to see caller ID indicate that it is Chuck Ellis.

"Hello, Chuck, I sure wasn't expecting to hear from you."

"Well, I hate to bother you, but I thought you would want to know. We found Sally Matthews dead in her cell this morning. She left a suicide note."

"How could that have happened, I thought she was under a suicide watch."

"She was, but evidently she had it well planned. She went to bed and went to sleep, then sometime during the night, she got into her wheelchair and used that patented device to stand. She must have used the remote to push herself forward so that her throat was pressed against the upper cot railing to cut off her air. Once she dropped the remote, there was no turning back, even if she had wanted to."

"That is so sad; I feel bad for her father and family. I do thank you for letting me know and will you please send me her father's address via a text. I want to send him a sympathy card."

"I will do that in just a few minutes. Have you started writing your book yet?"

"No, I'm on the way home from my honeymoon and will begin that project Monday morning."

CHAPTER 19

A WEEK HAS NOW passed since I talked with Chuck Ellis. Using my journals, I found it easy to write the bases for my story that I now think should be entitled, Killing Congress. But, I must admit there are forces out there telling me the story does not end here, and quite frankly, reminding me that it may be necessary to retitle the story to Killing America.

As an investigator, I learned long ago not to ignore the forces that pull you this way and that, but to give them appropriate consideration and respect. So, here I sit in my office trembling with both anxiety and anticipation, trying to organize the rest of the story.

Anxious, because I know that some will tune out any view contrary to their own, and yet, encouraged by the knowledge that an effort must be made to reunite us as a nation. Pay attention because the rest of this story will impact each and every one of you!

The five murder cases I investigated drew me deeper into the political arena than ever before. Some of the things I learned are even more alarming in retrospect than they were upon the first revelation. Here are some things that I heard from many different people from all political spectrums. I am confident that you have heard these thoughts expressed by those around you. "I am sick and tired of politics. Why does it have to be a win, win, win with no regard to ethics and morality? Why can't we focus on achieving better government through cooperation? My vote doesn't matter; they are going to do what they want too anyway. It seems like we have become our own worst enemy. I'm not even going to bother voting anymore."

If we are honest with each other, and I hope we will be, we can hear our own voices in at least one of the above comments. If that is correct, I submit that the future of our Democracy is in deep trouble.

If you bother to research failing Democracies, you will find that historians attribute such failures to the withdrawal of the people from the democratic process due to apathy and not being informed on the issues. So, when I say that the very future of our Democracy is on the downhill slide toward the abyss, I expect many to say, it can't happen, there are too many checks and balances in place. I will simply remind you of a quote from the second President of the United States, John Adams, Massachusetts born and Harvard educated who said, "Remember, democracy never lasts long. It soon wastes, exhausts, and murders itself. There never was a democracy yet that did not commit suicide." Then reflect on the things we hear people saying, things like those of a few paragraphs earlier. Do you see how the apathy expressed in those statements could become suicide notes, as relating to our political process?

Ask yourself, how do I feel about our Democracy? It has been in existence for 242 years and has undergone some bumps and bruises. We have heard bad things said about it, and we all have been influenced by those we have allowed to come into our country without regard to their commitment to Democracy. We assumed that they would assimilate to our culture, but many are hard at work trying to get us to change to their way of thinking.

Consider these somewhat harsh criticisms of Democracy:

Aristotle: "In a democracy, the poor will have more power than the rich, because there are more of them, and the will of the majority is supreme."

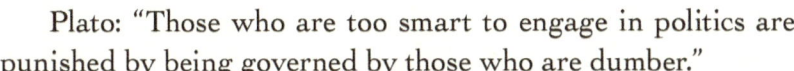
Plato: "Those who are too smart to engage in politics are punished by being governed by those who are dumber."

Benjamin Franklin: "A democracy is two wolves and a lamb voting on what to have for lunch."

Thomas Jefferson: "A Democracy is nothing more than mob rule, where 51% of the people may take away the rights of the other 49%."

Winston Churchill: "It has been said that democracy is the worst form of government except for all the others that have been tried."

Now, I ask will you join me in my stand with Churchill in his assessment above? I hope you will. But, I really believe that after you consider the following dangers that are threatening our Democracy, some of you will have to admit that you have been caught up in a trap that you have not even recognized. So, beware, I will be asking the question again.

Now, in the words of Paul Harvey, for the rest of the story.

In addition to the things we have already discussed, there are two very powerful forces out there attacking our Democracy. The first, but probably not the most dangerous, is socialism. Did I hear some of you scoffing that the cold war was over years ago? I hope not because I assure you that was just another battle, the war continues.

Let me ask you a question. What do you know about a man named George Soros?

I would like to introduce him to you by quoting from an article written by Dr. Michael S. Coffman, PH. D. on February 15, 2011, in NewsWthViews.com. He said, "Multi-Billionaire George Soros is waging a war on America's Constitution to transform the freest people in the history of the earth into a hedonistic/socialistic nation ruled by global governance.

"Almost unknown until recently, multi-billionaire George Soros has been quietly bringing down governments around the world. He has now turned his attention to the United States and

unleashed a firestorm of activity intent on destroying the U.S. Constitution and the U.S. dollar."

You should also consider that David Kuperlian, managing editor of WorldNetDaily.com and editor of Whistleblower magazine calls Soros a "God-hating atheist, a self-hating Jew, a capitalism-hating socialist, and an American-hating-globalists."

In 2004 Soros donated over 23 million dollars to the Democratic party and or its causes. It seems to me that there is some logic to why a socialist would support the Democratic party. After all, the liberal ideology supports more and more government, and it makes sense that it is easier to transition from Democracy to Socialism from the big government stage rather than the conservative stage.

But, what is now confusing is that Soros has supposedly switched his allegiance from the Democratic Party to the Republican Party. He has announced that to be true and he is now donating big bucks to Republican causes. It is certainly confusing, but what bothers me most is that I find no mention that he has given up his socialists' leanings. Until I see that I will not trust the man.

Let me make one more point regarding socialism. If you bother to go on the internet to look for differences in socialism versus communism, you will find the following statements. "Communism and socialism are umbrella terms referring to two left-wing schools of economic thought; both oppose capitalism. As an ideology, communism is generally regarded as hard left, making fewer concessions to market capitalism and electoral democracy than do most forms of socialism." The most common definition that I have found for Socialism is an economic system in which goods and services are provided through government ownership rather than through competition and a free market system. Therefore, it should bother you that in the 2016 Presidential Election, we had a candidate, Bernie Sanders, a self-proclaimed socialist seeking election via our democratic process. Which, if you believe he is a socialist, must mean that he intends to change the way goods and services are provided in our country and that he opposes capitalism? Yet, I did not hear anyone challenge him on his anti-democratic views. I find it frightening that we see people that have been elected to Congress, and who can run for the Presidency who openly define themselves as socialists. It should frighten all of you when you see our gullible young people flocking to his message like he was Santa Claus. Socialism will destroy the freedom that Americans have fought and died for since the foundation of this great nation. Wake up America!

CHAPTER 20

---◆◆◆---

FREEDOM

O UR COUNTRY WAS founded by those seeking freedom from oppressive government.

On July the 4th 1776 our founders signed the Declaration of Independence. In that document, they stated that "The history of the present King of Great-Britain is a History of repeated Injuries and Usurpations, all having in direct Object the Establishment of an absolute Tyranny over these states."

That document went on to charge the King with such acts as:

"He has forbidden his Governors to pass laws of immediate and pressing Importance."

"He has refused to pass other laws for the Accommodation of large Districts of People."

"He has obstructed the Administration of Justice."

"He has made Judges dependent on his Will alone."

For the above and other reasons our founders declared, "We, therefore, the Representatives of the United States of America, in General Congress, Assembled, appealing to the Supreme Judge of the World for the Rectitude of our Intentions, do, in the Name, and by Authority of the good people of these Colonies, solemnly Publish and Declare, That these United Colonies are,

and of Right ought to be, Free and Independent States; that they are absolved from all Allegiance to the British Crown."

Since the signing of the Declaration of Independence well over one million Americans have given their lives in defense of the United States of America. We have fought others, and we have fought among ourselves (losing over 625,000 in the Civil War) – some for righteous causes and some not so righteous – some we can be proud of and some we may hold our heads in shame. We aren't perfect, and we will disagree on many of the issues over which our people fought and lost their lives. We have achieved world supremacy in terms of military might, yet we are not infallible. But it is more likely that if America is ever defeated, it will be from within rather than by military power.

Crumbling from within has to be the most frightening issue before us today. We have become so divided as to actually hate one another for political views. All of us wrestle with the issue of government. Not so much, what kind of government, as with how much government.

Most of us intuitively know the liberty and government intervention scale, where no government represents chaos and 100% government results in tyranny. It is also easy to see the fallacy of "Place everything in the hands of the State," the Socialists urged, "and the State will take good care of us all." It is not as easy to find the maximum liberty we all desire.

It is the democratic process that is best suited to bring about the balance necessary to guarantee maximum liberty. If we are to achieve good government, it is essential that all of us work together. I remember reading somewhere, "The art of good government, is protection without oppression."

I wonder if those founding fathers are restless in their graves considering how members of the far-left clamor for more and bigger government, which we all know consumes valuable resources that have to be borrowed to pay the bill.

CHAPTER 21

A POISON DESIGNED TO KILL DEMOCRACY!

YES, MY FRIENDS, there is a danger out there that is far more sinister and deadly than our creeping toward socialism. It is a relatively new idea that has risen its ugly head, and so far, I have heard no one call it by its real name. I'm sure many are more qualified to do so than I am, but since no one else has spoken up, I will do my best to convince all of you of this looming danger. If it is not stamped out and eradicated, it will inevitably destroy our democracy.

The evil of which I speak is gaining popularity daily, and it is the idea of resisting the current administration in all that it tries to accomplish. Now we find Voices of Resistance Rallies occurring around our country. What's wrong with that, you say? I'll tell you what's wrong with it; it is anti-democratic. Our democracy, as defined in the Constitution, and stated in the simplest of terms, is based on the concept: we the people, in order to form a more perfect union voluntarily submit ourselves to be governed by our duly elected officials. Those of us who have served in the military or law enforcement, and or held elected positions have taken an oath to defend and uphold the Constitution of the United States. Indeed, every American citizen has an implied duty to defend and uphold our constitution. Therefore, one cannot say he's not my President or join in a resistance movement without declaring themselves to be a traitor to the Constitution of the United States of America. When the people elect a party or an individual, we are all duty bound to do our best to help that person or party succeed. Some of you are not ready to accept that, are you?

Let's look more closely at the concept of resisting the winning party. On the surface, the best thing I can think to say about the philosophy is that it is infantile, actually spoiled rotten childish would be more appropriate. The surface message is: I may have lost, but I am not going to let you enjoy your victory over me.

Examining the concept further will reveal it to be more than childish. Resisting the winning individual or party will ensure a weaker and less efficient government. Think about what will happen, if after four years the other party regains control, and now it is payback time. An analogy would be a football team with a perfect record at mid-season, the defense decides they are not getting enough credit for the team wins. So, the next week in practice they do everything possible to injure the offensive players so they cannot perform at their best for the next game. They lose that game. The offense then spends the next week devising ways to injure the defense and that leads to losing every game for the rest of the season. The resistance philosophy will result in a losing season for all, and it will lead to ultimate disaster.

Some may try to defend the philosophy by saying, oh, I don't mean resist everything they try to do, I just mean most. Even if you mean most or even some, resistance is still undemocratic. A closer examination of the resistance philosophy will reveal its' real message. The real message is: I am not willing to be governed by the will of the people, I am only willing to be governed by those who think and act as I do.

It is time to tell it like it is, to call a spade a spade, if you support the resistance philosophy you have, in my opinion, labeled yourself as a traitor to our Constitution. And you have become more dangerous than the likes of the Rosenberg's, who were executed, after being convicted of espionage. If, spying against your country, is serious enough to warrant a death sentence, what should the penalty be for murdering your country? There is no defense for the resistance philosophy, the numbers you may be able to gather into your fold not-with-standing, nor the political status of its' adherents cannot change the fact that the real message is both traitorous and murderous.

Yes, I am well aware that the losing candidate in the last Presidential Election has aligned herself with this evil philosophy with she declared, "I'm Part of the Resistance." Also, according to Paul Sperry, a New York Post writer, former President Barack Obama has implied that he is supportive of the philosophy. Here is what Sperry wrote, "When former President Barack Obama said he was 'heartened' by anti-Trump protests, he was sending a message of approval to his troops. Troops? Yes, Obama has an army of agitators ---numbering more than 30,000 --- who will fight his Republican successor at every turn of his historic presidency. And Obama will command them from a bunker less than two miles from the White House.

In what's shaping up to be a highly unusual post-presidency, Obama isn't just staying behind in Washington. He's working behind the scenes to set up what will effectively be a shadow government to not only protect his threatened legacy but to sabotage the incoming administration and it popular "America First" agenda."

Now, as I wind down toward the end of my story, I believe it is decision time for all of us. I have decided that I will stick to the title of my story as being that of Killing Congress. You need to determine where you stand on democracy. Do you see yourself as a member of the team who wants the best offense and the best defense, or do you want more credit for the side of the ball you play on? I will point out that although I have used a team analogy, the stakes are more than winning or losing, we are literally talking about life or death of our democracy here.

322 Second Street
Washington, North Carolina 27889

July 4, 2018

Dear Fellow American

As we celebrate the 242nd anniversary of our great country, I think it entirely appropriate to ask you again, as I said earlier that I would, where do you stand on democracy?

Before you answer, I will remind you again that when you resist the duly elected officials of our government you are really saying that you are not willing to be governed by the will of the people and you are selfishly proclaiming that you are only willing to be governed by those who think and act like yourself.

So, I make one final plea for all of you to join me in doing all within your power to stamp out this resistance movement. It is more dangerous than any serial killer of whom you have ever heard, and if we do not eradicate the movement in the very near future, someone else will eventually write the story of Killing America.

Sincerely,

Colt McLean, Lieutenant
Beaufort County, Sheriff's Department

THE END

ABOUT THE AUTHOR

G EOFF RETIRED FROM the Department of Defense in 1992 after serving more than 38 years. Over thirty of those years were in the Pentagon Building. As a member of the Senior Executive Service, he was called upon to testify before House and Senate Appropriations and Authorization Committees in support of several essential defense programs.

He and his wife Betsy have three daughters, twenty-one grandchildren, and seven great-grandchildren. They now reside in Winchester, Virgin.

www.ingramcontent.com/pod-product-compliance
Lightning Source LLC
Chambersburg PA
CBHW020327110726
47898CB00003B/777